"I'm fine."

For high school senior Parker Rabinowitz, anything less than success is a failure. A dropped extracurricular, a C on a calc quiz, a non-Jewish shiksa girlfriend—one misstep, and his meticulously constructed life splinters and collapses. The countdown to HYP (Harvard, Yale, Princeton) has begun, and he *will* stay focused.

That's why he has to keep it a secret. The pocketful of breath mints. The weird smell in the bathroom.

He can't tell his achievement-obsessed father. He can't tell his hired college consultant. And he certainly can't tell Julianne, the "vision of hotness" he so desperately wants to love.

Only Parker's little sister Danielle seems to notice that he's withering away. But the thunder of praise surrounding Parker and his accomplishments reduces her voice to broken poetry:

I can't breathe
when my brother's around
because I feel smothered,
blank and faded

nothing

For my good friend, Tom Davis,
who told me.

nothing
robin friedman

Woodbury, Minnesota

First Edition
First Printing, 2008

Book design by Steffani Sawyer
Cover art © 2008 by Stockbyte/Getty Images
Cover design by Gavin Dayton Duffy

Flux, an imprint of Llewellyn Publications

Library of Congress Cataloging-in-Publication Data
Friedman, Robin, 1968–
  Nothing / Robin Friedman.—1st ed.
     p. cm.
  ISBN-13: 978-0-7387-1304-5
  [1. Novels in verse. 2. Bulimia—Fiction. 3. Eating disorders—Fiction.
4. Self-perception—Fiction. 5. Family problems—Fiction. 6.
Jews—United States—Fiction.] I. Title.
  PZ7.5.F75 Not 2008
  [Fic]—dc22   2008008184

Flux
Llewellyn Publications
A Division of Llewellyn Worldwide, Ltd.
2143 Wooddale Drive, Dept. 978-0-7387-1304-5
Woodbury, MN 55125-2989, U.S.A.
www.fluxnow.com

Printed in the United States of America

Other Books by Robin Friedman

The Girlfriend Project

The Silent Witness:
A True Story of the Civil War

How I Survived My Summer Vacation:
And Lived to Write the Story

Parker

Puke.

My life is puke.

Literally.

I'm staring at a bunch of puke that used to be one chocolate French silk pie, one blueberry muffin, and two peanut butter cookies, all from Perkins.

"Parker!"

My sister, Danielle, bangs on the bathroom door. One fourteen-year-old sister, one seventeen-year-old brother, and one "cooperatively-shared" bathroom.

"I'm almost done," I call out as casually as possible.

Danielle, grumbling, goes away.

I have to flush twice to get rid of all the puke.

I carefully check my reflection in the mirror. My eyes are red and watery. I meticulously wash my hands and face in the sink, brush and floss my teeth twice, and

1

gargle four times with extra-strength, cinnamon-flavored mouthwash. Then I shove three wintergreen breath mints into my mouth. My pockets hold the world's record for wintergreen breath mints.

My sister, still grumbling, comes back.

"You're worse than a girl. It's time to come out and face your public now."

I check my reflection again. The eyes are blue-green; the hair's the color of "orange-blossom honey," says Mom, "like they make in Vermont."

It all fits the name Mom and Dad gave me—except for the dead giveaway of Rabinowitz being my last name.

I open the bathroom door.

"At last," Danielle sighs. "Time to make hearts break!"

I ignore this comment, shoot past her, duck into my room, and sweep my car keys off my desk.

It happened today because I'd hardly eaten anything.

I tried, but I just couldn't resist.

When I saw the Perkins, I jammed on my brakes so hard the UPS truck behind me nearly ended up in my back seat.

I hated myself for it.

But everything's okay now.

I undid the damage.

I flushed it all away.

Danielle

My big brother's
a breaker-of-hearts.

It's his talent
and hobby.

Ask any girl
at Livingstone High School.

Sometimes I wonder,
if that's it
or if it's
something else
completely.

I also wonder if
the reason people
like me
is because it's
the quickest way
to get to him.

Parker

I go downstairs. The house is dark and quiet, not a single Jerusalem of Gold sculpture or painting of the Dome of the Rock out of place. Mom and Dad are at the Jewish National Fund's Tree of Life Gala.

I walk to our four-car garage and get into my black Audi. My parents don't do Mercedes because of that lingering Jewish stand against the Nazis, but they make an exception for Audi.

I drive the few miles to Foxy's house. I guess he's been watching for me, because as soon as I pull into his driveway, he pops out of the front door.

"Yo," he grunts, sliding into the front seat, the whiff of his cologne making my nostrils flare. I crack my window even though it's February outside, pull off the driveway, and head to the party.

Jarod Fox and I have been friends since we shared a bar mitzvah date when we were thirteen. We're the same height (six foot one), our families belong to the same synagogue (Temple Shalom), and we take the same classes at school (AP Physics, AP Chemistry, AP Biology, AP Spanish, AP Calculus, AP Statistics).

Foxy plays trumpet in Jazz Ensemble, and is student

representative to the Livingstone School Board, vice president of our temple youth group, treasurer of Key Club, and managing editor of *The Cellar* (the school literary magazine). He's in Livingstone Chorale, Big Brothers/Big Sisters, and Make-A-Wish Foundation.

We're different in one way. Foxy has had girlfriends.

And the other thing.

Foxy starts messing around with the controls in the car, which I can't stand, but I let him do it anyway.

"Dude, when are you gonna let me drive this baby?" he asks, without expecting a reply, because he continues, "I'm asking out Tina Taylor the hot shiksa tonight."

"Mazel tov," I mutter; "congratulations" in Hebrew. Shiksa means "non-Jewish girl" in Yiddish.

"Now that Spaz's committed," Foxy goes on.

I frown. "I know."

Pete Spazzarini isn't Jewish. He's vice president of National Honor Society, vice president of Key Club, vice president of Student Council, and on the forensics team. He's in Big Brothers/Big Sisters, Make-A-Wish Foundation, and Model UN, and he doesn't have a problem with being called Spaz.

How are Spaz and I different? He likes building his college resume.

We arrive at the party. It's at the end of a dirt road,

more a compound than a house, with outbuildings and sheds. I guess it's an old farm of some kind, one of the last remaining pieces of open space in New Jersey. The actual party seems to be in a barn.

I park on the front lawn between two trees, and Foxy and I nonchalantly make our way to the barn. Once inside, we stand around trying to look cool, mostly wondering what we should be doing. I slide three more wintergreen breath mints into my mouth. It takes a lot of energy to look cool.

Spaz suddenly materializes with Amber Weinstein, one of the hottest girls in school, who's clinging to his left arm as if her life depends on it.

"Ready to hoe down?" he asks.

"Yee-hah," Foxy replies dully.

"I'd pay real money to see you dance, Parker," Spaz says.

I wish I could think of something brilliant to say in response to him in the three seconds I have before he and Amber walk away, but all I can manage is a grunt.

Spaz and Amber go off to a hay-strewn area that's doubling as a dance floor. They start kissing, Amber enveloping Spaz's mouth with such passion I feel like I should look away.

"That girl thinks the sun rises and sets in his pants," Foxy observes.

I wonder what it would be like to be with a girl who liked me as much as Amber likes Spaz.

The real me.

"Wanna dance?" It's Julianne Jennings, a shiksa and vision of hotness.

"I don't dance," I answer.

Julianne takes my hand and leads me to a set of rickety stairs. I have no idea where we're going. We climb to a loft of some kind. A hay loft, I guess. It's pretty dark up here, and lots of other couples have the same idea.

This is our routine. Julianne and I have hooked up at every party since our senior year started last September.

Julianne finds a free spot literally *in* the hay, pulls me down, and soon we're making out furiously. I don't want to stop, and we don't come up for air for a long time. But, when we do, Julianne isn't happy.

"When are you gonna actually ask me out, Parker?"

I can feel her long eyelashes against my face. I can also hear the hurt in her voice. I think of Amber and Spaz—the way she kissed him, clung to his arm. I want that.

"Is it because of your family?" she asks.

It would be easy to use this as an excuse. "No … It's just … " I start to say.

Julianne sits up and picks hay out of her hair. "I give up," she sighs.

I watch her leave. I feel sick.

But there's nothing left inside me to throw up.

Danielle

They call Parker
"McDreamy."
Like the brain surgeon on that hospital show.

He's been hearing
since first grade
that he "doesn't look Jewish."

Whatever that's supposed to mean.

Parker doesn't watch that show
or any TV at all.

He's got three hours of
extracurricular activities
and three hours of
homework
every night.

I know he wants to get into
Princeton.

Because that's where Dad went.

And Harvard and Yale are too Jewish.

Parker

People think I'm cool, but I'm really not. I just pretend, so they'll like me.

Julianne is in this category. She thinks I'm the coolest guy around.

I get up and look for her, but the place has gotten a lot more crowded. I can't find her anywhere.

The sick feeling inside me gets worse until it feels like panic. And, all of a sudden, I'm thinking about chocolate French silk pie.

I walk out of the barn, trudge across the front lawn, and make my way to the house. The front door's locked, but the sliding doors in the back are open. I slip through the doors, find my way to the kitchen, and rummage around as quietly as possible. I seem to be the only one here. There's got to be people upstairs, but the first floor's dark and empty. I don't see or hear anyone.

I open a walk-in pantry and hit pay dirt. There isn't a pie, but there are cereal boxes and bags of potato chips and jars of peanut butter.

I devour an entire jar of peanut butter, a whole box of cereal, a bag of potato chips, and four glasses of milk.

I'm stealing this food. I can't believe I'm stealing this food.

I focus on the food, only the food, eating the food as fast as possible, not Julianne storming off, not stealing, not anything except eating the food.

But it doesn't last.

I know what I need to do. The mere thought disgusts me, but it's better than the alternative.

Vomiting is vile, but for all its revolting effects, it's all that stands between me and regaining control.

I find a bathroom, gag myself with my finger, and hurl into the toilet bowl. Everything comes up in a hot, disgusting rush.

I'm ashamed of myself, but when you think about it, there aren't any other choices.

I won't be fat. I won't be a failure.

My mouth is sore. I can't go back out there without brushing my teeth. I start rummaging like crazy, looking for someone's toothbrush, and I find one, and I use it.

My throat burns and I feel itchy all over. But I accept the pain. It's worth it.

I'm tough. I can endure this.

I hesitate just before opening the door. What if someone has noticed the missing food? What if someone's waiting to use the bathroom?

I promise myself I will never do it again.

———

When I return to the party—after thoroughly dousing myself with mouthwash and wintergreen breath mints—I still can't find Julianne.

I end up in the hay loft anyway, for the second time that night, with a hot girl, whose name I don't know, from the Teen Tzedakah Project.

Danielle

Parker and I have Teen Tzedakah Project
on Sunday mornings at the JCC
(that's Jewish Community Center).

Two years ago,
Dad gave a "major gift" to the Emergency Israel Campaign
and they renamed the JCC the Rabinowitz Family
Campus.

My parents are machers,
"big shots,"
people with connections.

Me and Rachel Weiss (that's my best friend)
are on postsecret.com
when Parker gets in from his party.

We offer him mint jellybeans

as he passes by in the hall.

"Fat free," Rachel says,
extending a handful to him.

Rachel lives and dies for seeing my brother.
We've been best friends since fourth grade
even though she's so the typical JAP
(that's Jewish American Princess)
without even trying.

Parker stares at the jellybeans for so long

I wonder if they remind him of something.

"Next time," he says, smiling.
"Ohhhh," Rachel murmurs.
Involuntarily, of course,
and turns pinker than bubble gum ice cream.

I roll my eyes.

Parker doesn't even have to try
at pretty much anything
but especially
at getting girls to
fall madly in love with him.

It must be nice
to have that kind of power.

Not that I would know
anything about it.

"How was your party?" I ask him
when we're in his car the next morning
on our way to the JCC.

"Okay," he answers with a shrug.
"It was in a barn."
I want to know more.
I want to know if Julianne Jennings was there.
Parker's been her crush forever.

Parker turns on the radio
which means he doesn't feel like talking.

Tzedakah is Hebrew for "charity."
It's part of tikkun olam,
"repairing the world,"
"making the world a better place."

Mostly, it looks good on college applications.

Parker

They have bagels with four kinds of cream cheese (lox, veggie, walnut-honey-raisin, and olive-pimento) for us in Room B, where the Teen Tzedakah Project meets, but I just have coffee, black.

That hot girl from last night is talking to Amber Weinstein.

"The UN should be abolished," she says, tossing her long black hair. "I totally refuse to do Model UN no matter what my college consultant says. I don't need it for the University of Chicago anyway."

"That's not an Ivy," Amber says. "Isn't that a safety school?"

"Well, it's not HYP, if that's what you mean," the hot girl says huffily, then walks away, still tossing her hair.

Aaron Rosenthal, the JCC's youth coordinator, tells us to take our seats. We sit down around the big table, Foxy and I at our usual spot at the far end. A lot of people yawn discreetly. I wonder if Aaron thinks we're hard partiers, always tired on Sunday mornings, but I'm never in bed before 1:00 a.m. on weeknights either.

Aaron ignores the yawnings and tells us the money we've raised so far has bought textbooks for third graders

15

in Israel at a school for Ethiopian immigrants. He reads us a letter from the mayor of Ofakim, our sister city, thanking us for our generous donation.

"We hope you will come and visit us in Ofakim," he reads. "And see for yourself what a difference you've made."

Not likely. And not because of Middle East violence. Because of the importance of this question: "Will it get me into college?"

Aaron puts down the letter and leads us in a discussion about responsibility, but that seems beside the point, and I don't contribute anything. He ends the meeting with his usual *"Am Yisrael chai!"* That means, "Long live people of Israel!" or something like that. Chairs scrape, everyone gets up, some people head back to the bagels. The hot girl pours herself more coffee. She drinks it black, too.

Aaron comes over to me and says, "Parker, been meaning to talk to you. *New Jersey Jewish Ledger* is starting a teen section in the paper and they want an editor. Interested?" He pauses, then adds, "Your dad is actually funding this project."

I can't say no. I can't say no to being Parker Rabinowitz.

Besides, for me, the important questions are doubled:

Will it get me into college?

Will it make Dad happy?

Danielle

Parker drives me, Rachel, and Foxy home.
Rachel's so excited she's actually
bouncing up and down in her seat.
After all, she's in an Audi with two seniors.
Two hot seniors.
"Wanna stop at Starbucks?"
she asks hopefully.
Nobody from school can see us here in Parker's car.
But if we were at Starbucks
with Parker Rabinowitz and Jarod Fox ...
Now that's a coup.
Parker meets Rachel's eyes in the rear-view mirror
and she lets out a little gasp,
breathless, I guess, at his attention.
I know he'll say no.
He's still got temple youth group, Torah enrichment,
Make-A-Wish Foundation,
and peer leadership today.
"Sorry, Rachel, maybe another time."
He grins.
She melts.
"I wonder if we'll hear anything this week," Foxy says.

This is all seniors talk about.
Who applied where, who got in where,
who didn't get into their first-choice school
and has to go to a state school.
Foxy won't say which schools he applied to.
Nobody reveals that.
But I know Parker's are HYP.
Harvard, Yale, Princeton.
It's bad now that both Harvard and Princeton
dropped their early decision programs.
"I know a kid with a formula," Foxy says
in a voice barely above a whisper.
Parker looks up sharply,
first at Foxy, then at me.
Livingstone High School eliminated class rankings a year
    ago, but it's still highly valuable information.
Knowing how to get it
is like knowing who to get drugs from.

Parker

According to the information Foxy gets from some math-club geek, I'm number one in our class. Which is great.

But Amber Weinstein, of all people, is a too-close second. Which is not great. Not to mention hard to believe.

"Because Amber can't 'act smart,'" Danielle says. "Because she's a babe."

I snort. "It's the twenty-first century, Danielle."

"Of all people, you should understand, Parker."

"Why?"

Danielle fixes me with a hard stare. "Because it's okay for guys to be smart, just like it's okay for guys to be slutty."

"And that's the way it should be," I say lightly.

Danielle rolls her eyes.

I gaze down at the scribbled note Foxy passed along to me.

"All I need are a couple of B's on my quizzes in AP Calculus and I'm toast," I mutter. I get a tickle in my throat.

Amber Weinstein should focus less on being smart and more on being a babe.

Or, at the very least, stop going out with Spaz.

It looks like Danielle wants to say more, but it's almost time for dinner. Besides, I've wasted enough time today, first with Foxy, now with Danielle. I've got a paper due tomorrow in AP Spanish, plus a lecture tonight at the synagogue on "Emotional Parenting."

And since I'm a youth representative, I can't not go. Just like I can't drop any activity, even the ones I hate, because I need them for college.

———

At age eleven, I set my sights on Princeton.

I was reading by the time I started kindergarten. I've been a straight-A student since first grade. I've had a college consultant since I was a freshman.

It's a competitive world and I want to do something with my life. I want to feed the hungry, and house the homeless, and stop global warming, and eliminate poverty and AIDS and war.

I want to succeed. I want to make Dad happy.

Mom makes one of my favorites for dinner, chicken

enchiladas, and it's absolute torture for me not to eat as many as I want. I know I can get rid of them later, but I have to watch it. I don't want to get caught.

"How's calculus?" Dad asks.

I take my time in answering this question, because I'm not sure how much I can fudge it.

"It's getting pretty hard," I say, reaching for my water glass. I've been really thirsty lately.

"Anything worth doing is hard," he says, smiling, but it's not one of those smiles that makes you want to smile back. "Nothing's easy, Parker. And anything less than success is failure."

I say nothing in response. What can I say? I've been hearing this all my life.

"Parker works so hard," Danielle pipes in.

I turn to her in both shock and admiration. Danielle's braver than I'll ever be.

Dad smiles again. "He should work hard. If he wants to make something of himself. It's tough out there."

"Please pass the guacamole, Parker," Mom says pleasantly, and if I weren't feeling so miserable I might've laughed.

None of us talk for several minutes. Mom, in her role as Passive Bystander, fills the silence with news from Sisterhood's Paid-Up Membership Dinner about who's getting divorced, whose kid got accepted to medical school, who's moving to Boca.

I pick at my food, keep my head down, and try to make myself invisible.

Later that evening, before the lecture at the synagogue and instead of writing my AP Spanish paper, I sneak away to the twenty-four-hour drive-through at McDonald's, order two Big Mac meals, sit at the furthest end of the parking lot, and wolf down everything in less than seven minutes.

Then I go home and hurl it into the toilet bowl.

Danielle

How Mom and Dad
can sit in this auditorium
and listen to "Emotional Parenting"
without feeling like
it's directed specifically at them
makes no sense to me at all.

"Wanting our kids to be educated is a Jewish value," the
    speaker says.
"From their toddler years we instill in them that the de-
    fining moment of their lives will be the college ad-
    missions process, that success equals admittance to a
    top-tier college."
He pauses and looks around the room slowly.
Everyone suddenly sits up straighter.
"The Jewish community needs to redefine success.
It isn't getting into the best schools.
It isn't making a lot of money."

Parker started seeing his college consultant
when he was a freshman,
but Mom and Dad haven't talked to me about it yet.

Sometimes I want them to
drive me hard too,
as hard as they drive Parker.
Why am I not worth that kind of attention?
What does Parker have that I don't have?

But, most of the time, I'm glad they act
as if I don't exist,
because I don't think Parker's life
is a whole lot of fun.

Or is it?

I keep looking over at my brother
to see his reaction
to the speaker's words.

But his expression is
emotionless
like a mask
like it was at dinner.

Parker

Track is one of the extracurricular activities I hate.

I've been pushing myself harder lately and things have started to hurt. Still, I tell myself I can take it. Besides, if I can't hand Dad calc on a silver platter, at least I can deliver track.

We're doing laps outdoors today even though the wind is bitter cold and my nose is manufacturing nonstop snot icicles. Coach has his obnoxious whistle in one hand and his trusty stopwatch in the other. He barks at us like one of those Marine drill sergeants in the movies. I just ran a 200 meter, but Coach gives me barely enough time to catch my breath before making me do another one.

I haven't eaten much today. No breakfast or lunch, just a Red Delicious apple right before practice.

When I pass the bleachers, a girl waves at me.

I squint into the sunlight. It's Julianne.

Julianne!

I smile, then frown, then smile again.

Is she here to see me?

What if I do something lame?

I wave back and do a half-lap past her. I feel dizzy. But this time it's different. This time I see explosions dancing in front of my eyes.

Am I going to pass out?

No. Not now. Not with Julianne here.

I slow down, try to breathe more deeply, but it's too late.

The explosions get brighter and bigger. Then everything goes pitch black.

I crumple to the squishy red track, right on top of a brightly painted number five.

Coach hurries to me, Julianne rushes over, the whole team arrives.

I can't look at anyone.

I am a failure.

———

"Are you sure you're okay?" Julianne asks.

"I'm fine."

We're leaning against my car in the school parking lot.

Coach called practice over and sent everybody home. Then he pulled me aside and made me lie down while he gave me a lecture on taking care of my "temple" and being a responsible athlete.

"I didn't mean to ... distract you, Parker," Julianne says. "I just ... I wanted to say hi."

"You didn't distract me," I say.

I reach out without meaning to, and Julianne responds immediately, stepping into my arms. The next thing I know, we're kissing urgently. Julianne pulls back but stays in my embrace, looking up at me, waiting.

"Parker?" she prompts.

"Julianne, I ... I ... I'm sorry."

Spaz and Foxy can have girlfriends because they've got nothing to hide.

Julianne blinks furiously, then squirms out of my arms, sniffling.

I floor it to Dunkin' Donuts and inhale a dozen doughnuts, then get rid of everything, poof, down the drain, bye-bye.

Danielle

The bathroom's
been smelling funny lately.
I'm not sure what it is.

Why do Parker and I
have to share a bathroom
in such a big house?

Because Mom says we
need to learn to live
"cooperatively."

Whatever that's supposed to mean.

It makes sense, I guess, when you say it.
It's totally different when you have to live it.

Parker

I make it through the day without eating anything but an apple.

Yellow Delicious.

Danielle

Jews technically don't celebrate
Valentine's Day.
I mean, it's named for a saint and all.
I think he died defending true love.
Or something like that.

I wonder how he would feel
if he knew his martyr's death
revolved around heart-shaped boxes of bonbons.

It's kind of hard not to
celebrate Valentine's Day at Livingstone.
Each year, the junior class
sells roses to raise money
for the United Way.

Sounds good, doesn't it?

Then why does Valentine's Day
make me sick to my stomach
as I wait in homeroom
for the cart of roses
at the front of the room
to be given out to everybody?
Well, no, not everybody.
Some people get nothing.

I get one red rose from
Rachel
and one white rose from
Parker.

Parker gets eighteen
red roses
that morning.

Parker

Amber Weinstein throws a party and we all go.

Julianne chooses this exact time to punish me for my indecisiveness. She's wearing the tightest, shortest micro-mini I've ever seen on a girl, and whenever she spots me, she flirts with the nearest guy around.

It kills me. It really does.

Everyone's either paired themselves off to hook up or they're a couple to begin with. Foxy and Tina have gone upstairs. Spaz and Amber are making out like crazy—Amber using Spaz as a chair—in the middle of the living room. When Spaz sees me watching them, he gives me the thumbs-up sign. I want to respond with the finger.

"So, who do you like, Parker?" he asked me last summer.

"Amber Weinstein," I replied.

"Julianne Jennings has the major hots for you, ya know," he said.

"I know," I said. "She's hot too."

"So who would you pick?"

"Amber Weinstein," I said again.

I walk over to where Julianne's hanging all over some creep from Newark Academy.

"Julianne, can I talk to you?" I ask.

She appraises me coolly. "I'm busy, Parker."

I stiffen. She's dismissed me, and it stings worse than a slap across the face. But I don't give up.

"Please," I say.

She swallows. "Okay."

We go into the laundry room. I pull her into my arms. "Are you trying to make me jealous?"

"Yes," she says with a smile.

"Well, it's working."

"Cool."

I lean forward and kiss her, and she kisses me back, but she pulls away in the middle.

"I can't, Parker," she whispers. "I want … more." She stares into my eyes, waiting.

I know that if I don't do this now, if I let Julianne walk away from me—even though it's close to two o'clock in the morning—I'll end up at Kings, pulling cheese doodles,

33

onion rings, and Doritos off the shelves. The thought of doing this excites me, makes me feel good, makes me feel great, and I want to do it.

Desperately.

I let Julianne go.

Danielle

Rachel wants us to try out
for pom-poms
or flags
or whatever
those dumb things are
that involve jumping,
screaming,
and acting like a moron
in a short skirt
and boots with tassels.

"It'll look good on our applications,"
she says.

"Maybe I don't wanna
go to college," I say.
"Maybe college is evil."

Rachel gasps
as if I've said something
absolutely horrifying.

But I mean every word.
Especially the evil part.

Parker

I have an appointment with Myrna Katz and Associates after school.

"Call me Myrna," she said on the day we met, my freshman year. "You don't look Jewish at all, Parker, so what do you want to major in?"

The sign on her desk read:

Ask Me About My 98% Track Record
Of Getting Your Child Into
The Nation's Most Elite Universities

Myrna Katz and Associates (I never did meet the Associates) was my new college consultant. Her office was in a building above a Japanese restaurant in downtown Millburn. ("Before you leave, be sure to try the sushi platter downstairs," she'd say every time. "The spicy salmon rolls are to die for.")

Mom and Dad came with me to that first meeting, and I wore a tie. I was excited, and eager, to be working with a college consultant.

"I want to major in pre-med," I replied. "I want to be a neurosurgeon."

Myrna nodded. "A nice Jewish doctor." She leaned forward. "Tell me, Parker, is that what you really want? Or are you doing it to make Mom and Dad happy? Because if you're doing this for anyone but yourself, you're going to fail miserably. It's a long, hard road, and I need you to be 200 percent committed. Can you give me 200 percent for the next four years?"

I was thunderstruck. Mom let out a cry of surprise and Dad started to say, "We don't—"

Myrna held up her left hand, and without even looking in Dad's direction, said, "I believe I addressed that question to Parker. What's your answer, Parker?"

Well, truth was, I didn't know. What I wanted and what they wanted never diverged. They were inseparable—tangled together. I was seven years old when they bought me my first toy stethoscope.

"I'll give you 200 percent," I said.

Myrna nodded for the second time. She took out a purple folder and began writing in it. "For the next four years, we'll meet twice a month. I want you to take every

AP class your school offers. They don't offer AP Gym, do they? No, I guess not, but I'm working on it, because do you know what you could do with a 5.0 weighted GPA? You'll sign up for one sports activity, two extracurriculars, one community project, and two Jewish projects every semester. Don't ever make any summer plans without consulting me first. And when it's time for your testing"—she looked up from her folder—"that's PSATs and SATs, mind you, we'll meet every week."

I stared back at her wordlessly.

"Congratulations, Parker," she said. "You're one of the chosen."

Four years later, her words still haunted me.

Chosen for what?

"Well, hello, Parker," Myrna says when I arrive. "Still haven't tried the sushi platter after all these years, have you?"

I shrug and take my usual seat in front of her desk, the sign about her "98% Track Record" staring back at me. The first meeting was the only one Mom and Dad were allowed to attend. Myrna insisted we meet alone— just her and me—after that.

"This is all about trust and you're going to have to trust me," she told them. "And, in return for your trust, I promise I will get Parker to the top."

The top of what?

"So how's it going?" she asks.

"Fine." Standard answer.

"We're almost there, you know, all your hard work is about to pay off big time."

I grunt.

"Parker," she says, leaning forward. "It's almost over. We don't want to trip at the finish line, do we?"

I say nothing in response.

She gazes at me for a few seconds in silence, and when she speaks again, her tone is softer. "I know it's hard, Parker. I know it's a lot of pressure. But I'm only doing what you asked me to do. Remember when you scored 1570 on your SATs and you were so proud of yourself and I told you to re-take them? Well, you got a perfect 1600 after you re-took them. I know what's best for you, Parker."

I shake my head. "No, you don't."

Her mouth falls open. "What? My job is to get you into the school of your dreams. The rest is up to you."

I exhale loudly. I'm so tired of this. All of it. "I was asked be the editor of a new teen section at the *New Jersey Jewish Ledger.*"

"You already have too much," Myrna says. "It sounds terrific, but you don't need it. You said no, right?"

"I can't say no," I say, and it feels great to say this out loud, to impose this weight on someone else for a change.

Myrna cocks her head to the side. "You don't need it, Parker. You have too much already."

"What do you know about what I need?"

I get up, seeing red—no, seeing the pie case at Perkins.

"Parker. Hold on. Wait!"

I walk out.

———

I drive toward the industrial area by the bridge, past go-go bars and girly clubs, toward a Starbucks in a massive shopping center overflowing with SUVs and minivans. A guy in an orange vest mutters to himself as he rounds up Wal-Mart shopping carts into impossibly long blue snakes. Moms drag screaming kids to Sam's Club for bulk bargains. I swerve to avoid a near-collision with a white van hemorrhaging Girl Scouts in front of the Rag Shop.

My cell rings. Myrna Katz and Associates. I shut it off.

I order three coffees—venti, black—and head home, taking the long way past miles of yellow-brown cornfields. When I get there, I find Danielle and Rachel in our home-theater room.

Dad had our cavernous basement remodeled a while

back to look like one of those old movie palaces you see in glossy coffee-table books. There's a huge silver screen, a state-of-the-art projector, a blow-your-eardrums-away sound system, framed movie posters of classic films like *The Wizard of Oz*, *Gone With the Wind*, and *Casablanca*, and even an old-fashioned, red-and-gold popcorn cart that Mom rescued from a rotting boardwalk pier in Asbury Park. Mom also found three flea-bitten rows of faded, blue-velvet seats in a cow town in Montana, with gilded arm rests carved to look like lion's heads. They were restored to their original blue splendor by a movie-seat expert in Brooklyn.

It's cool, actually, though it's never accomplished Dad's goal of having weekly Family Movie Nights. Danielle and I like to use the room. It's dark and quiet, and the seats are comfortable. Foxy and Spaz are always asking me to throw a party here.

"Lights Out and Make Out City," Spaz says.

"That could be our theme," Foxy adds. "Girls like themes."

"If I had a home theater, I wouldn't let it go to waste," Spaz tells me once a week, most obnoxiously.

"Ohhh, McDreamy," Rachel murmurs when I walk in.

"Hey," I say.

"Hey, yourself," Rachel replies. "We got nomination

forms for Senior Sex Symbol today. You're so going to win, Parker."

I give her a forced smile. Senior Sex Symbol is an annual fundraiser for our local chapter of the American Red Cross. I notice Danielle eyeing one of my coffees. I should offer it to her, but I got three for a reason. I have a calc quiz tomorrow; it's going to be a long night.

"Well, see ya later," I say, and go up to my room.

I turn on my cell. Three messages from Myrna.

I turn it off again.

Danielle

"Your brother's so cool and so hot!"
Rachel says
as we're standing in front of the bulletin boards
deciding what to join.

Everything on the bulletin boards
already has my brother's name
and time served on it, in an ink only I can see.

Amnesty International
Chess Club
Digital Art Club
Environmental Club
Future Physicians
Inner Voices
Mock Trial
Peer to Peer

Peanut Butter and Jelly Club
Philosophy Club
Ping Pong Club
Science Olympiad
Yearbook Club

"Do you know, like, how lucky you are?"
Rachel asks me.
"To be his sister? That everybody knows it?"

I want to tell Rachel I'd give anything
to go to a school
in which my brother didn't come before me.
It's been that way since nursery school at temple.

How can a person think something is so great
when in reality it's so bad?

I'd change my name
to something even more Jewish-sounding
like Sadie Perlmutter
just to have the chance
to do something in which
I wasn't being compared to Parker Rabinowitz.

Or how about
Parker-Rabinowitz's-Little-Sister-Who-Otherwise-
Doesn't-Have-A-Name?

Parker

I have trouble with my calc quiz. It's my last class of the day, and I have to run to youth group afterward, then peer leadership, then Big Brothers/Big Sisters. I call Myrna on the way.

"Parker, thank goodness, I was going to give it till the end of the day, then I was going to get in touch with your parents. I haven't lost a client yet and I'm not about to lose you. So, whatever it is, we can work it out. Talk to me."

"It was nothing," I reply flatly. "I was just a little tired yesterday. I'm sorry."

"I know there are a lot of pressures on you, Parker, but we're almost at the end."

"I know."

"Are you sure that's all it was?"

I hesitate. "Yeah."

"All right, then, I'll see you at your next appointment. Call me if you need me."

Click. Dial tone.

I know Myrna's a busy woman with a million other clients, but I wish she'd asked me that just one more time.

———

Instead of heading to youth group, I drive to the development where Julianne lives. It's old, probably even historic, and the houses are the kind that architecture magazines put on their covers. Julianne's has fat white columns and a giant sloping lawn. When I get there, though, there are no lights on at her house, and I realize I'm displaying stalking behavior by being here unannounced like this. This isn't the kind of neighborhood where people would hesitate to call the cops to report a strange car. That's all I need, for Dad to get a call from a desk sergeant asking him to bail me out.

So I leave, but I make myself say it out loud: "I'm going to ask out Julianne."

Danielle

"Who do you think Parker
secretly crushes?"
Rachel asks me
after we vote
for Senior Sex Symbol
in homeroom.

I almost want to say,
"You, honey,"
just to shut her up.

Parker doesn't secretly crush anyone
or if he does
he hides it pretty well.

I remember the first time
Parker brought a girl home

for his eighth grade dance.

Mom took him shopping
at Sam's in Livingstone
for the perfect suit.

His date, Dianne Levy,
wore lavender-lace ruffles.

I helped Parker choose a corsage
from the catalog at the florist's.
Bicolored orchids with a spray of ribbon.

Mom told him he had great taste.

She snapped pictures
of him trying to pin it to Dianne's dress
in front of the river-rock fireplace in our living room.

The obligatory, before-the-dance, parental photo shoot.

Dad got impatient,
I guess,
because he snatched the corsage
out of Parker's hands
and tried pinning it
to Dianne himself.
When that didn't work, he shook it hard.

A shower of blossoms

bled across
Dianne's lavender-dyed satin pumps.

Her lower lip trembled.

Parker gazed down at the floor.

I started to say, "Dad ... "

Parker said Dianne avoided him
for the rest of the year.

I didn't go to my eighth grade dance
because nobody asked me.

Parker

We get our calc quizzes back and there's a big fat red C on mine.

I have track and peer leadership and Key Club, but I get that tickle in my throat again, and I go to the parking lot, and I get in my car, and I drive.

I end up in Julianne's neighborhood again. Only this time she's sitting outside, on her porch, wrapped up in a blanket. I can't get myself out of my car fast enough, and I trip over my feet and make a complete fool of myself, but I don't care. When she sees me, she starts for the house.

"Julianne! Julianne!" I call like a lunatic, racing toward her.

She turns toward me, but holds her arms against her chest protectively as if I'm a mugger who's going to hurt her.

"What do you want from me, Parker?" she asks when I frantically climb the porch stairs and stop in front of her.

I lower my head. "I don't know."

"Do you want me ... to be your girlfriend?"

Her tone is so hopeful, and I can't help feeling like I don't deserve it. I take a step forward, then stop myself.

"I'm ... I'm afraid," I say.

Why did I say that?

She looks at me questioningly. "Afraid? Of what? Of me? I'm not going to gouge your eyes out, Parker. I'm harmless. Really."

I smile a little. "I'm ... I'm afraid you won't like me."

The real me.

She laughs. "Not like you? But I do like you. I like you a lot."

"I like you too, Julianne," I say. "I think ... that ... I ... I love you."

Oh. My. God.

Julianne gazes at me for ages. Then she steps forward, slides her arms around my neck, and kisses me.

———

I've missed track, and if I don't get myself back to school, I'll miss peer leadership. I drive to Spaz's house instead.

The doorbell's one of those longish-tinkling ones, the

kind that chimes a few opening notes from a forgettable old song. Spaz answers it himself. He's still in his Best Buy uniform, which means he just got off work.

"Hey," he says, letting me inside as if it's the most natural thing in the world for me to be on his doorstep.

We sit down on a zebra-print sofa in the living room. Without any warm-up, I say, "I asked out Julianne."

"About time, dude."

"Yeah," I say, not sure why I found it necessary to drive all the way here and give Spaz this piece of information.

"If you'd waited much longer, someone might've beat you to it," he says with a half-smile.

So that's it. Like those animals on nature shows peeing on stuff to protect their turf.

"She's not Jewish," I say, trying to imagine me and Spaz locking horns or antlers or whatever we'd lock if we were animals going at it on those shows.

He shrugs. "Neither am I."

That has nothing to do with anything. I think of the way Amber kissed Spaz at that party in the barn, and my hot new shiksa suddenly feels like a consolation prize. Or is my new status with Julianne some kind of strategy?

"I'm a big believer in carpe diem," Spaz says.

"Seize the day?"

"Yup."

I wish I could set aside our rivalry for just one minute to have a real conversation with him. "How do you do it, Spaz?" I murmur.

"How do I do what?"

"You know … pressure."

This is the closest I've ever come. When Spaz doesn't answer, though, I lose my nerve.

"Forget it," I say, feeling enraged with him—and myself.

"No, hold on, dude, I know what you mean," Spaz says. "It's, like, my parents were freaking, 'cause my college consultant says I'm not gonna get into my first choice. But we decided that's okay 'cause it's more important for me to be happy." He pauses, and when he speaks again, it's in a voice devoid of its usual boredom. "You're gonna be valedictorian, Parker. Your SATs are perfect, and you've got a legacy at Princeton."

I clearly hear the admiration in Spaz's words, and even the envy, and for a moment I feel victorious. But then I fumble.

"Princeton's picky about Jersey people," I say.

"Okay, so you'll go to Harvard or Yale," he says, and it's still in that same envious-defeatist-desperation voice.

I shake my head. "No good."

He sits up and gestures wildly with his hands. "You're

putting the pressure on yourself, Parker. What's the problem?"

They say guys don't like to talk about their feelings, but Spaz is actually one guy who does. Still, I change the subject.

"Ever do any tutoring, Spaz?"

"You need help with something, Parker?"

I bristle. That word.

"I don't need help with anything," I say, surprising myself with this automatic belligerence. It's like a reflex, like when the doctor hits your knee with that stupid hammer. Beyond control.

"Is it calc?" Spaz persists.

"It's nothing," I say, getting up. "Forget it."

———

I could still make Key Club, but I decide to just go home. Mom's at the house when I get there.

"Parker?"

"Mom?"

"What are you doing here?" we both ask at the same time.

We stare at one another silently, a few feet apart, as if we're facing off in an old Western.

"How was school?" Mom finally asks, falling back on the old standby.

"Fine," I reply, doing the same.

I stand there, and instead of quickly climbing the stairs to my room, shutting my door, shutting her out, I wait. For what? For small talk about Sisterhood? For an explanation as to why she's home? For an actual conversation in which my mother takes a normal interest in me?

I study Mom. And I realize this: she looks old. I don't usually pay attention to this kind of stuff, but now I see things I've missed. Wrinkles around her eyes, a droop in her smile, almost a resignation in her expression.

Is my mother unhappy?

What makes her unhappy?

Dad?

If my father makes me miserable, and if he makes Danielle miserable, doesn't it logically follow that he makes Mom miserable too?

Well, that's her business. I've got my own problems. I start to go.

"Parker?"

For a moment, I panic, thinking she's discovered something about me. But that's impossible. I'm careful.

"A girl called for you," she says.

Well, now, this is cryptic. Lots of girls call me. Usually they call my cell, but sometimes they call the house.

"Julianne?" I ask.

Mom nods. And smiles. "Is she your girlfriend?"

My cheeks get hot, but I don't know why this embarrasses me. "Yeah," I say. "She's my girlfriend."

I'm still getting used to saying that.

"You've never had a girlfriend," Mom says.

I'm shocked Mom would even know this. Maybe she pays more attention than I thought.

"Yeah," I answer. "She's the first."

Mom grins. Me getting a girlfriend has made her happy? "I want to meet her. Maybe you could bring her by."

"Um, okay."

"Maybe we could have her over for dinner."

Over my dead body.

"She's busy," I say, and Mom senses the shift in my tone immediately. Well, it's pretty obvious. The thing I'm not expecting, though, is her reaction. Her eyes get misty.

Well, you know what? Too bad. There's no way I'm subjecting Julianne to a family dinner. I'll pull out all my toenails with my front teeth before I do that.

"Why are you home anyway?" I ask, my voice cool and unfriendly.

Mom blinks furiously, and I feel horrible that I will

probably never, ever be able to have a normal conversation with her because of all the mileage between us.

"We have something to tell you," she whispers. "Later. At dinner."

She turns to go.

———

I call Julianne back, and she's so thrilled to hear from me, so sweet to me, that I feel as happy as Mom felt about me having a girlfriend.

I feel so great after I hang up with her that I'm positive Julianne will cure me.

I'm in a fantastic mood when I come down to dinner.

"I hear you have a girlfriend."

Dad's beaming at me just like Mom did.

If I had any idea all it took to liven things up around here was me getting a girlfriend, I would've done it a long time ago. Why is my getting a girlfriend a cause for celebration? I can't remember the last time Dad was so cranked about something I did.

I crave his approval like junk food. It's an emptiness that never gets filled. No matter how much I try to fill it, load it, stuff it, cram it, it doesn't feel full.

It's a feeling of perpetual ... nothing.

Dad clears his throat and says, "Kids, we need to tell you something."

"Breast cancer."

It lingers at the table like a bad smell.

I haven't heard much of my father's short speech—I've tuned him out—but I immediately latch onto those two words.

Danielle and I both turn to Mom with worry on our faces. I may have issues with my mother, but I don't want her dying on me.

"It's not your mother," Dad says, and for the first time in my life I'm not scared of him, because he looks tired and old and...defeated.

"It's me."

———

I'm in my Audi and I'm going almost a hundred and I don't care because I have to get to the supermarket.

NOW.

Pieces of conversation from dinner buzz in my head like white noise from a radio stuck between stations.

"One percent of breast cancer patients are men."

"I'll undergo the same treatment women do."

"Surgery, chemo, radiation..."

I've never, ever, ever, ever heard that one-percent statistic, much less knew men could get breast cancer.

Leave it to Dad to scale new heights of medical territory.

It occurs to me, as I'm frantically pulling packages of Oreos, pretzels, and Sun Chips off shelves, that this is really inconvenient. Every time I need food, I have to jump in my car and get it.

Why don't I buy more than I need right now, and store it somewhere?

I fill my shopping cart to the top. At the checkout line, the cash register blinks $137.38 at me. Did I buy that much? I'm lucky to have enough cash to cover it. I could use my credit card, but that bill goes directly to Dad.

At home, I hide my food behind a bunch of old shoe boxes in my closet. As I fall asleep that night, it isn't thoughts of Julianne that lull me to sleep. It's knowing I have a stash in my closet.

Danielle

I don't know what to talk about first!

Parker getting all the attention at dinner
again
because he has a girlfriend?

He didn't mention Julianne
being not Jewish.

It's nice, actually, that she's
not a JAP like the rest of them.

She doesn't wear shirts that say
Supermodel
across the chest in pink rhinestones
or short-shorts that say
Hottie
across the butt.

You're probably wondering
why I'm babbling about my brother's harem
instead of talking about
Dad
but to be honest
I'm in shock.

A man with breast cancer?

I don't know
what to think
or
what to do
or
what to say.

It's funny,
well, not funny in a hahaha way,
but funny in a weird-funny way,
that everyone always wants to be
different from each other,
unique,
special,
one of a kind.

I want it too,
I want it a lot,
but not like that,

not that different,
not that unique,
not that special.

That's more like being alone.

Parker

I devour the American Cancer Society's web pages on What Is Breast Cancer in Men?

My dad's breast cancer is called a breast adenocarcinoma, and the type he has is called a ductal carcinoma.

Not that these words mean anything to me.

Breast cancer is one hundred times more common in women. In 2007, 450 men died of breast cancer in the United States. And 40,460 women.

Talk about an elite group.

Danielle

I ask Mom how she met Dad
even though I've heard
this story before
like a zillion and a half times.

We're stuffing blue gift bags
with silver tissue paper
dotted with tiny stars of David
in the living room
for Fashion for Philanthropy,
Mom's charity group
to support wounded soldiers in Israel.
Every time I crumple up the silver tissue paper
I see my reflection in it,
distorted.

"It was at a youth group dance at our temple,"

Mom says, smiling at the memory.
"He was the only boy in a suit.
Some of the boys wore ties
and some of the boys wore jackets,
but your father was the only boy in a suit."

"So?" I ask.

Mom looks right at me,
her hands frozen in place,
tangled up in silver tissue paper,
but her eyes are seeing something
in the past.

"So I knew he was a serious boy,"
she says.
"I knew he would take things seriously."

She frowns.

"Too seriously."

We don't talk for the rest of the stuffing.
My reflection in the silver tissue paper
with the tiny stars of David
gets more funny-looking
the more I look at it.

My dad's name is David too

like the star
like the king.

I keep trying to picture him
dancing with Mom,
but I can't.

It doesn't make sense for Dad
to do anything that doesn't involve
making money
or bossing people around.

Parker

I'm out of money, so I go downstairs to see Dad.

Usually he pays me every week, but he must have forgotten.

I'm not used to him hanging around the house so much, doing nothing. He sits in his study downstairs, behind his big desk, and stares out the window for hours.

I knock on the door even though it's open, and my dad looks up, surprised, and I almost turn around and leave because my knees have gone weak all of a sudden.

Dad says, "Come in, Parker, sit down." Not in an unkind way.

So I do, and as I get closer, I notice my dad looks old, like Mom. And ... tired.

He's wearing a green bathrobe. I don't think I've ever seen him undressed. Or, if I have, I can't remember it.

I sit down in the big chair in front of his desk, but before

I can decide whether I want to go through with this or not, he says, "Please don't tell anyone...about this. I've been meaning to talk to you. I can only imagine what people will say."

He's asking me to keep a secret.

He cares about what people will say.

Dad opens a drawer in his desk, unzips a black leather pouch, and pulls out a fat stack of crisp and fresh bills-from-the-bank. I can actually smell the money from where I'm sitting. It smells clean and new, energizing, like a jolt of caffeine.

"Here," he says, handing the stack to me.

"Thank you," I say, accepting it automatically. I resist the urge to run the stack under my nose for a closer inhalation.

It's more than usual, and I realize it's a...bribe. But, then, it's all a bribe, isn't it?

Dad winces. Is he in pain?

"How are your grades?" he asks, and some of the old fire creeps back into his eyes, and just like that, I'm back to being Jell-O again.

"Great," I answer in a whispery voice, even though the big fat red C on my calc quiz has probably tied me with Amber Weinstein.

Dad nods. "I'm counting on you, Parker."

Counting on me for what?

Danielle

After school I sit in our home-theater room
and watch *The Music Man* by myself.

The Music Man is a Technicolor
song-and-dance fest
about a place in Iowa
where people make chocolate fudge and
grow pretty flowers on trellises and
nothing bad ever happens.

Mom took Dad to the cancer center
again
and Parker's out
again
and I'm alone
and I wish
I could jump

into the big screen
and live in River City, Iowa,
with the fudge and the flowers
where nothing bad ever happens.

I hear footsteps
and suddenly Parker's
standing in front of me,
staring at the huge tub of buttered popcorn in my lap.

"Hey," he says.

"What are you doing here?" I ask.
"I thought you had forensics."

He smiles. "What—do you know my whole
schedule by heart?"

"Yeah," I say. "Actually, I do."

"It was cancelled," he says.
He studies the screen.
"*The Music Man*?"

I nod.
And hope.

He stands there,
weighing his options.

Homework?

Julianne?
Or watching a movie with his little sister?

He plops down next to me.
I want to do a dance
but I offer him popcorn instead.

"No," he says, shaking his head vigorously.

Parker

Julianne's going to cure me.

I'm in love. I know it.

When I go to her locker after school, she jumps into my arms and wraps both of her legs around me. She doesn't seem to care about all the people staring at us and I don't either. I hold her tightly off the floor and kiss her frantically.

"Can I watch you today at track practice?" she asks after we've pulled apart.

I run my mouth along her neck. "I don't know…I might get distracted with you there, imagining all the things I want to do to you."

She giggles. "Want to meet me at the diner after?"

I freeze.

Julianne bites her lip. "Is something wrong, Parker? Did I do something wrong?"

"No, no, no," I say, bringing her hands to my mouth and kissing them. "It's just…"

"How about you come over tonight?" she asks, rescuing me.

Danielle

I mention the funny smell in the bathroom to Parker,
and he acts all weird about it.

Why?

What is it?

A few hours later,
there's a new smell
in the bathroom.

It's nice.

Misty Mountain Strawberry,
according to the pink-and-red spray can
on my side of the sink.

Parker

I eat two bananas for lunch and successfully don't pig out on Mom's horseradish-crusted London broil, one of Dad's favorites.

Danielle

Dad has a paintball-corporate-retreat fest
in the Poconos with his office every year.

I've always wanted to go.
It sounds like fun.
I wonder if he'll take me this year.

"I have really good aim," I say,
when I come down to visit him in his study.

"If you aim at nothing,
you'll hit it every time," he replies.
"My aim is awesome," I say.

"Ready, aim, aim, aim, fire!" he answers.

Sometimes Dad can get a little annoying
with all his "life sayings,"
but I still want to do paintball with him tomorrow.

Parker

Dad wants me to play paintball with him.

"It'll be awesome!" he says as we stand in the living room putting the finishing touches on our protective-clothes-layering. I'm so puffed-up with protective layers I feel like the Michelin Man.

Mom frowns at us. "David, really, Parker doesn't have time for this nonsense."

"Sure he does," Dad replies absently, tightening a scarf around his collar. "And it's not nonsense. It's a team-building activity."

"He's got homework and midterms and papers," Mom goes on. "He's got serious work to do. He doesn't need to be running around the woods like a crazy person."

"He needs a break from the books, Beth, he needs fresh air and exercise."

Danielle studies us from under half-closed eyes. She's

still in her nightgown—it's just after dawn—and I wonder why she even bothered coming down to see us off.

"Parker gets enough fresh air and exercise," Mom counters, her voice growing shrill. "He's on the track team, remember?"

I wish they'd stop talking about me as if I'm a wind-up doll they can just plop down wherever they want.

Dad ignores Mom's comment and turns to me. "Ready?" he asks. "Let's move out, pardner."

Mom throws up her hands. "You're being completely unreasonable, you know."

"Bye, honey," Dad responds, giving her a quick kiss.

We move out.

First stop: Starbucks.

———

The line for Starbucks spills out the door even at this godless hour.

Unshaven guys read *The New York Times* while women in yoga pants stare into their cell phones.

I get my usual three coffees—venti, black. Dad gets a tall cappuccino—hold the foam—which I guess makes it technically a latte.

"Do you always drink so much coffee, Parker?" he asks as we head back to my Audi.

"Um, yeah," I answer, feeling suddenly self-conscious about it.

"What—are you secretly putting in time at NORAD or something?"

It occurs to me that Dad doesn't know how late I'm up most nights, and frankly, I'd rather keep it that way.

In fact, I worry Dad will grill me the whole way to the Poconos about my life, but after just two minutes on the road, he's off in La-La-Land, snoring away.

———

I get lost twice, and by the time I pull into the paintball place I've been driving for almost two hours and could use a serious nap. Dad wakes up as I bring the car to a halt in the gravel parking lot.

"Perfect timing," he says, stretching. He claps me on the back. "You ready?"

I shrug.

"It'll be awesome," he says.

We exit the car and walk across the parking lot. There's a hut on the other side with a neon sign that says:

Poconos Paintball Inc.
Groups Welcome

Everyone from Dad's office is already inside the hut, crowded around an ancient-looking coffee machine, looking like an army of puffed-up Michelin Men.

"Hey, everybody, glad you could make it," Dad says. "Anyone have trouble getting here?"

People murmur, shake Dad's hand, make small talk, and otherwise act like caffeine-deprived weekend warriors.

Dad puts his hands on my shoulders. "This is Parker, everybody, you remember him."

More murmuring, more handshaking, a few nods.

Dad makes his way to the counter, which is manned by a guy with the kind of white beard Santa would envy. "Any release papers I gotta sign throwing all my civil rights in the toilet?"

I stand to the side by myself as Dad confers with the Santa guy behind the counter. If you were to ask me what my father did for a living, it would be hard to give you an accurate answer. He isn't in the Jewish mafia or anything, but Dad's businesses are definitely on the mysterious side. I know they have something to do with direct mail—that would be junk mail—and marketing, web design, advertising, and sending out loads of spam.

Whatever it is, it's hugely successful. There was a time

when Dad used to talk to me about taking over the business one day, but the idea of me at medical school erased that plan for good.

Dad finishes with Santa and we're led to a room in the back, where we get fitted for helmets and are handed our paintball guns.

"Pink today," Santa says, holding up a pink-colored ball.

Groans of disgust and disapproval.

"Pink?" Dad exclaims. "Oh, really, come on."

Santa shakes his head. "The contract clearly stipulates there is no color selection."

"We'll see about that," Dad grumbles. "You'll be hearing from my attorney."

Santa looks unmoved. He opens a door for us; we trudge out of the hut and into the woods.

———

The first hour, nothing happens.

A lot of aimless wandering. A lot of aimless cursing.

The second hour, Dad gets talkative. We all started as a big group, but now it's just the two of us. Dad peels off his gloves.

"My hands are sweating bullets," he mutters. "I feel like a fat sweat hog."

I take off my gloves, too. All these Michelin-layers are making me warm.

Dad looks at my hands, then at his own. "I built my whole business with these babies," he says, holding them up. "Bare hands. Out of our basement in Brooklyn just after you were born."

I've heard this before—dad's rags-to-riches story about how he made something from nothing.

"I made something from nothing," he goes on. "I didn't have it handed to me on a silver platter like you kids do." He shakes his head. "Kids today. Between college consultants and armies of private tutors and cell phones that talk back to you…"

There's a sharp THWACK, and the middle finger on my left hand feels like it's suddenly on fire.

I let out a howl of pain and stagger backward, losing my balance and falling to the ground. A telltale splatter of pink covers my hand. I was hit.

"Parker!"

Dad reaches for me, but his face contorts and he doubles over, holding his stomach and moaning.

We both lie there, wounded.

Danielle

The doctor says Parker's finger
isn't broken.

Mom doesn't care.

"What if he'd been hit in the head?"

"We were wearing helmets," Dad mumbles.

"Did the helmet cover his eyes?" she snaps.
"What if he'd been hit in the eyes?
No—more—paintball!"

Dad isn't eating much.
Neither is Parker.
They've been like that
all through dinner.

They called us on Mom's cell yesterday

while we were having lunch at Martini's.

I'd ordered the roasted butternut squash bisque
and three-mushroom tomato-basil quiche.
Mom had the Moroccan turkey salad.

It was after our sea salt facials at B'Cara Salon & Spa.

After lunch, Mom was going to take me shopping at Saks.

A girls' day out.

But we never got there.

Parker

I have to wear a big bandage on my finger for a week or two. At least it's my left hand. Besides, injury equals sympathy in the girl department.

"Poor Parker," Julianne says when she sees me. She studies my bandaged finger, then kisses it twice.

I take her to the movies that night and we spend the whole two hours making out in the darkened theater.

Afterward, Julianne asks, "Want to grab a bite to eat?"

"Um, well, okay," I mutter.

"Is something wrong?" she asks.

"No, nothing's wrong," I say.

I hold her hand on my thigh as I drive to the Livingstone Diner, letting my thumb rub circles into it.

Julianne orders a double-bleu cheeseburger with seasoned curly fries. I order a garden salad with fat-free Italian dressing.

Julianne stares at my salad, then takes my hand and doodles inside my palm with her finger. "Are you okay, Parker?"

I hesitate, but just for a second. "Yeah," I say. "I'm fine."

I pull my hand back, pick at my salad, and keep my head down.

We don't talk.

Danielle

The results are announced during homeroom
over the speakers by Amber Weinstein.
Parker wins Senior Sex Symbol.

"Ooooh," Rachel squeals, nudging my elbow.
"I told you he'd win!"

I don't say what I really want to say, which is:
I may not be a straight-A student or
president of Student Council or
president of Key Club or
president of National Honor Society or
president of youth group or
editor of *New Jersey Jewish Ledger*'s new teen section or
a track hero
or Senior Sex Symbol.

But I'm somebody, too.

Parker

Dad asks me to go to minyan with him.

My family's not religious, though we are "actively Jewish." Rabbi Goldwasser calls it "cultural Judaism."

We celebrate all the Jewish holidays, support Israel, and give money to Jewish causes. But we don't keep kosher, go to synagogue regularly, wear kippot on our heads, or keep the Sabbath.

A minyan is a quorum of ten people required to start a prayer service. It used to be ten men, but now it's ten people, including women. Our synagogue has a daily minyan every morning at 6:00 a.m.

When we arrive, I see I'm the youngest person there, by at least seventy years. Well, I guess Rabbi Goldwasser and Dad aren't ready for Medicare either, yet.

We find seats in the hushed sanctuary and open our prayer books. My Hebrew's actually pretty good, thanks to way too many years of religious school. The light that slants through the stained glass window gives everything in the room a pink aura, the same color as the paint that nailed me on Sunday.

Dad winces. I glance at him, remembering how he doubled over on the ground during paintball. He wasn't hit.

"Are you okay?" I ask.

"Yeah," he answers faintly. "I'm fine."

The same lie I told Julianne.

Everyone rises to their feet, so I stand too. Dad remains seated.

When I sit down again, he leans over and asks, "Have you lost weight, Parker?"

"No," I say.

I spend the rest of the minyan staring straight ahead of me in this room of Jewish guys named Irving, Norman, Mortimer, and Harry—not Parker—and women named Gladys, Millie, Rose, and Mildred—not Amber.

When the minyan ends, the rabbi comes over and thanks us for coming. He shakes my hand, then shakes Dad's.

"Have you lost weight, David?" he asks.

Danielle

Why doesn't Dad
take me to minyan?

I feel mean today
so I barge into Parker's room
even though we're not supposed to do that
because we're supposed to
"respect each other's privacy."

"You've got it all," I say.
"You're gorgeous,
you're smart, and
people pay attention to you."

He gazes at me for a long time in silence.

I get goose bumps suddenly
because it feels like

he's about to tell me something
really, really important.

But he only says,
"You wouldn't understand,"
in the tiniest little baby voice,
and this voice is so sad,
it's the kind of sad you can
actually feel inside your chest.

I put my hand over my heart
and let out a little moan
and run back to my room.

I don't feel mean anymore.
I feel like giving Parker a hug.

But I stay in my room
and visit postsecret.com.

If I had the guts, the postcard
I'd send would say:

Sometimes I wonder
what my life would be like
if I were an only child.

Parker

Every time I think about calc, I want to throw up, which is strange, because I'm already throwing up.

Danielle

Here's another secret
I'd send
to postsecret.com:

I didn't vote for my brother
for Senior Sex Symbol.

Not because he doesn't deserve it.

Because it's about time
he lost something.

Parker

I get a D on our next calc quiz.

At the drive-through window at Taco Bell, I order three steak burritos and three orders of cheesy potatoes.

Danielle

Amber Weinstein crowns Parker
Senior Sex Symbol in the cafeteria.
Parker lowers his head so she can
put the sparkly gold crown on him.

"Take your shirt off," says the photographer
from *The Roundup*, our school yearbook,
pointing her camera at him.

"Take your shirt off!" everyone chants.
Foxy whistles. Spaz hoots.
Julianne covers her mouth and giggles.

Teachers roll their eyes.
This is a Livingstone tradition.
It's all for a good cause.

But Parker looks exactly like

that deer we almost hit
when we were coming home from an
apple-picking trip last year.

He shakes his head
and walks off the mock-stage.
Just like that.

"What's McDreamy's problem?"
a girl whispers behind me.

I could tell her to shut up.
Or butt out.
Or buzz off.

But I can't answer her question
because I don't know either.

Parker

I go to Julianne's house almost every day.

Today, we're making out as usual in her room, Julianne lying on top of me. She tugs on my shirt and says, "Take this off."

I freeze. "No."

She giggles. "Don't play hard to get with me, Parker, like you did with your adoring public yesterday."

"No."

She asks disbelievingly, "You don't want to take your shirt off?"

I shake my head vigorously.

"Why not?" She leans close and makes her voice sexy. "How am I supposed to run my hands all over you?"

I would take everything off if she wanted. But not now, during the day, when she can see everything—like in the cafeteria, where everyone could see everything.

Julianne frowns. "What is it now?"

"Nothing," I say. "It's just … can we close the blinds?"

She giggles again. "You're shy?"

"Um, yeah, I'm shy."

"You? But you've got a great body."

Great body? Why does everyone keep torturing me about this? I know I need to lose weight. I know I'm a failure.

I kiss her, hoping it will take her mind off my shirt, but when I'm done, she says without missing a beat, "I feel like you're keeping something from me. You're so secretive."

"I'm sorry," I say. Then, "I'm not keeping anything from you. Honest."

Liar.

Big fat liar.

Julianne gazes deeply into my eyes. Looking for the truth in there? Well, forget it. I learned a long time ago how to keep my eyes from revealing my secrets.

"Okay," she finally says. "So, if I close the blinds, you'll reveal your gorgeous pecs to me?"

I smile a little. "What about you? It's only fair."

She grins. "No, just you."

"Not fair. What about equality between the sexes? Women's rights? Double standards?"

She laughs. "I love you, Parker."

Julianne loves me.

I need to eat.

———

It wasn't always like this.

In the beginning, all I wanted was to lose a little weight.

"Did you know that when we meet someone for the first time, 55 percent of their first impression of us is based on our appearance?"

It's true. It's one of Dad's favorite "life sayings."

Half of all Americans are on diets, according to a study by Weight Watchers, but only 5 percent succeed in losing weight and keeping it off.

It was last year at Thanksgiving. I ate so much, so fast, I felt nauseous afterward. I actually made myself feel sick.

"Quite the feeding, eh, Parker?" Dad commented as I sat at the table trying to hide my nausea. "The average American adds eleven pounds to his already-fat body between Halloween and New Year's."

He pinched my stomach. I flinched.

I excused myself from the table, locked myself in the bathroom, and vomited into the bowl. It wasn't intentional.

But as I flushed away our Thanksgiving dinner, it dawned on me. I'd gotten rid of the problem. I'd eaten as much as I wanted, but I'd made the calories disappear.

By vomiting them, I'd undone them. I'd undone any damage caused by my overeating.

I could eat as much as I wanted.

With. No. Consequences.

I had the magical protection of vomiting.

Danielle

Mom and Dad are at the cancer center
again.

Parker's never here.

I live in a house where
there's a lot going on,
too much going on,
except no one ever talks about it.

Today, my postcard would say:

Sometimes I wonder
what it would be like
to live in a poor country
where, instead of worrying about stupid stuff,
like going to college,
what clothes are cool,

and what other people think,
you have to worry about real stuff,
like eating,
having clean water to drink,
and keeping flies off your face.

Parker

The offices of the *New Jersey Jewish Ledger* are behind the Rabinowitz Family Campus by the Hirsch Memorial Library. I'm three minutes early for my appointment with Aaron Rosenthal.

"Hey, Parker," he says, leading me into a conference room and placing a stack of newspapers in the center of the table. "Have you lost weight?"

"No."

"So, the first order of business here is a name," he says, pushing the stack of newspapers toward me. "They want a teenager-oriented name for this section. Something hip like Fresh or Ink or Fresh Ink. I know teenagers like to leave letters out of words. Razr and Grl. You know."

No, actually, you don't know. You don't have a clue.

"So, what's the most important issue facing teenagers today?" he goes on. "What do teenagers want to read about? Hey, by the way, can I count on you to chair our Kosher Food Collection next month?"

How much do they think they can keep dumping on me?

I ignore Aaron and page through the stack of newspapers in front of me.

There are stories about Iraq, Hamas, Hizbullah, hate crimes bills, AIPAC, Nazi-era diaries, a Holocaust film series, and anti-Semitism in Europe.

Those are interesting stories, but there aren't any about getting into Princeton, flunking AP Calculus, male breast cancer, or vomiting.

There are no stories about pressure, losing weight, parents, or shiksa girlfriends.

What's the most important issue facing teenagers today?

What do I want to read about?

Where do I start?

Danielle

I read in a magazine a while back
that we're called "millennial kids"
because we were born in the 1980s and 1990s.

Our parents waited a long time to have us.
Some, like Mom and Dad, needed help.

We get a lot of attention
because our parents have fewer of us
than their parents did.

We were the first generation to wear bike helmets
and get strapped into car seats.

We join a lot of groups
and do a lot of volunteering.

Our parents expect a lot from us.

Parker

Mom makes another of Dad's favorites for dinner, sweet and sour meatballs, with lemon pie for dessert.

"Mmmm," Dad says, though he's barely made a dent in any of it. "Let's pack some of these puppies for St. John's Soup Kitchen. There's a run tomorrow night at the synagogue."

"Not for you," Mom replies. "There's an appointment at the cancer center for you tomorrow night."

Dad frowns. "So? We can do both."

"No, we can't."

He turns to me. "I bet Parker can handle it. What say you, Parker, about taking your old man to the cancer center tomorrow after making a meatball run to the synagogue?"

"Leave Parker out of this," Mom snaps. "He's got enough going on."

I glance at Dad, then at Mom, then back at Dad.

I want to say yes, of course. And I want to say no.

Besides, Mom's right. I have two papers, two exams, three meetings, and one quiz.

I'm in danger of flunking calc, losing my number-one spot to Amber Weinstein, being fat, not being valedictorian, and not getting into Princeton.

At least my father has a cancer center to go to, a place where people help him get better.

I wish I had a not-feeling-like-a-big-fat-nothing center to go to.

Danielle

Minyan
paintball
now the cancer center.

I
am
invisible.

After dinner, I go up to my room
and write a postcard to my brother:

Dear Parker,
I hate you.
I love you.

I hate your perfectness.
I love your perfectness.

I hate the way you make me feel.

I love the way you make me feel.

For just one minute
I wish I could feel
what it would be like to be you.

I bet it's
something.

Love (and hate),
Danielle

Parker

"So, how's calc, dude?" Spaz asks on our way to meet Foxy at study hall in the library.

I shrug. What can I say? I'm not sure if Spaz's trying to be helpful or harmful.

"I know what you need," he says. "A change of scenery."

I snort. I don't see how "a change of scenery" is going to lighten my extracurricular overload, get me an A in calc, cinch my acceptance to Princeton, make Julianne stop being suspicious of me, make Danielle stop being jealous of me, cure Dad, cure me, or solve any of the world's problems, but it's hard not to bite when Spaz gets enthusiastic about something.

"Where to?" I ask.

"Red Bank," he answers immediately. "The Hippest City in New Jersey. We'll triple date. It'll be awesome."

The last time something was supposed to be "awesome," I ended up with a nailed finger. But that bandage is off now, and like I said, it's hard not to go along with Spaz. Besides, maybe he's right. Maybe I could use time away from classes and calc quizzes and Aaron Rosenthal and minyan and Myrna Katz and Associates.

"The only thing is how do we get there?" Spaz asks as we spot Foxy at one of the round tables in the back.

"We going on a road trip, dude?" Foxy asks.

"Roger," Spaz answers. "I could borrow the minivan."

"No way," Foxy huffs. "We can't go suburban lame. Let's rent something."

I peer at the row of computers in the middle of the library. "Let's book something right now."

We pull three chairs around one of the free terminals and look up limo-rental companies.

"Oh, baby," Foxy says as a picture of a stretch Hummer appears. "Now we're talking."

Spaz smiles from ear to ear. "What do you think, Parker?"

"I think," I say, typing away. "It's ours."

Danielle

I write another postcard to Parker:

Dear Parker,

Do you ever wish
you could start over
from
nothing?

I do.

I even love the way the word sounds.
Nothing.

No shadows
no boundaries
no edge.

Just a

huge
unfilled
empty
nothing.

My life is so crowded
with
you.

Everything I touch
has your fingerprint on it.
Everywhere I go
has your footprint on it.

My life is
smeared
with your
presence.

I
long
for
nothing.

Love,
Danielle

Parker

I pull out my copy of my application to Princeton from the bottom of my drawer, and take a look at it.

It's all there. My whole life.

All my accomplishments, successes, honors, activities, memberships, leadership positions held, trophies awarded, A-pluses earned ... all reduced to a careful listing shaped by Myrna Katz and Associates.

I worked my butt off for every word in there.

Looking at it now, I can't believe how meaningless it all was ... empty, pointless, a big fat nothing.

Danielle

Parker's going on an all-day road trip with his buddies
    tomorrow.
They even rented a stretch Hummer.

He was a little worried about
what Mom and Dad would say about it,
but it's not like they're ever home anyway,
waiting up for us, you know?
They aren't even going to be around that day.
They're going to be at the
Iris Applebaum Forty-One-Mile Motorcycle Run
for Juvenile Diabetes.

Besides,
Perfect Parker
can do no wrong.

Oh.
I feel mean when I think things like that.
Parker's not a bad brother.

I heard Mom and Dad arguing last night.
Mom said Dad was trying to pretend
nothing was wrong.
Dad said nothing was wrong.

Mom said, "You have cancer!
You should be resting,
not riding around on a motorcycle!
You can't pretend nothing's wrong!"

Dad said, "Don't tell me
what I have,
what I should do,
or what I shouldn't do."

That's when I turned up the volume on the TV.

Rachel and I are going to watch
three seasons of *Scrubs*
downstairs in the home-theater room
and eat raw chocolate-chip-cookie dough.

It's not as glamorous as everyone else's plans
but it sounds pretty great to me.

Parker

The stretch Hummer arrives right on time. That extra wad of money Dad gave me—the *bribe*—more than covered the cost. And there's more where that came from.

Spaz, Foxy, and I pile into the waiting car. It's huge, and the chauffer's so discreet I barely notice his presence. The distance between where he's sitting and where we're sitting is so large I can hardly make out the back of his head. Foxy pushes a button to activate the screen between us and he disappears entirely.

We head to Tina's house to pick up the girls, not talking or even looking at each other during the ride there. I think we're all feeling unsure about this triple-date change-of-scenery. But when we arrive, the girls are waiting on the driveway, and as they climb in, laughing and talking, the place gets livened up considerably.

Julianne wraps herself around me, and when I peek at

Foxy and Spaz, I see their girlfriends are doing the same thing.

"It's funny, isn't it, that we're all Jew-non-Jew couples," Amber observes.

I guess that's true. Me and Julianne (Jew and non-Jew), Spaz and Amber (non-Jew and Jew), Tina and Foxy (non-Jew and Jew).

"We could switch," Foxy says. "Do a little swinging."

Tina punches him in the shoulder.

"Oww," Foxy protests.

"Why's it so important anyway?" Julianne asks. "It seems kind of silly."

"It's not important to me," Spaz chimes in.

"Cause you're not Jewish," Amber says. "My parents think it's really important. They want me to marry a nice Jewish doctor."

"They want me to be a nice Jewish doctor," I say.

Everyone laughs. Amber turns red.

"Do they know?" Tina asks.

"Yeah," Amber says. "They're not happy about it."

"Mine aren't so thrilled either," Foxy says.

"What about yours, Parker?" Spaz asks.

My story's a minefield for all kinds of reasons, but I wonder if Spaz's testing me again. Isn't Amber enough? Does he want Julianne too?

"They don't know yet," I say, which is the truth. "At least, I don't think they do." Also the truth. "But I think they'd be okay with it." A half-truth.

Julianne snuggles against me. I could've asked out the hot girl from the Teen Tzedakah Project whose name I still don't know. I could've asked out Amber before Spaz beat me to it.

I'm not the rebel type. At least, I hadn't been up to now.

———

Two hours later, we pull into Red Bank. Roving groups of rich Rumson kids mill around Broad Street in front of Zebu Forno. We get out in front of Starbucks.

We walk around—stroll past Old Monmouth Candies and stop to look at a display of cashew brittle, peek inside Carlos O'Connor Mexican Restaurant ("Bring Your Own Water"), check out the Dublin House and Broadway Diner. We wait outside on a bench as the girls look inside Coco Pari.

Foxy stretches. "I feel like majorly pigging out today."

"Me, too," Spaz says.

I say nothing.

"You know what the number-one topic is with guys?" Foxy asks.

It's not sports or girls; otherwise, he wouldn't bring it up.

"Dieting," he says when neither of us responds.

I don't like where this discussion is heading.

The girls bound out of the store.

"This is so much fun," Tina says, folding herself into Foxy's lap.

I hold out my arms to Julianne and she nestles into mine.

"Hey," Amber says, making a frame with her hands. "We should take a picture."

Foxy grins. "Three Hot Geniuses Flanked by Their Adoring Wenches."

Amber snorts. "Three Stooges, maybe."

A gleam comes into Spaz's eye. "Which one of us is the best?"

Amber shakes her head. "Oooh, dangerous territory, male ego and all that."

"Come on, woman, we can take it."

Amber scrunches up her face and studies us. "Well, Parker's definitely the hottest, no contest."

"Parker?" Spaz sputters. "Who's the most brilliant?"

"Parker."

"Tough crowd," Spaz grouses. "Don't I get anything?"

"Loudest? Craziest? Most annoying?"

"Best body?" Spaz persists.

Amber sighs. "Parker."

I jump to my feet, nearly knocking Julianne to the ground, and rush down the street.

I hear Spaz's voice. "Hey, Parker, we were just joking around."

Amber calls, "Parker? I didn't mean to ... "

Why do they have to tease me about my body?

"What's wrong, Parker?" Julianne asks, following me.

"I want to be alone," I reply.

Julianne's eyes tear up. It stops me, but just for a second. I cross the street and keep going. I don't realize Foxy and Spaz have come after me until they're both right behind me.

"Parker, wait," Spaz says. "I'm not sure what just happened."

"Are you okay?" Foxy asks.

"You shouldn't say stuff like that," I mumble, stopping in front of Fameabilia. "Stop bringing it up all the time." I absently pop two wintergreen breath mints into my mouth.

Foxy stares, but Spaz asks, "What's with the breath mints, Parker?"

I shove the breath mints back into my pocket. "Look, forget it, okay?"

Danielle

Parker doesn't feel like telling me
anything about Red Bank.

He's lying on his bed staring at the ceiling.
He's been that way for an hour.

A part of me wants to help him
because there's something obviously
bothering him.

Another part of me wants to strangle him
because he has so much going for him
but he doesn't know it. Why?

So I decide I'm going to tell him
what I did while he was off
in his stretch Hummer with
his harem and big-shot friends.

"We watched three seasons
of *Scrubs*," I start. "And we each
ate an entire roll of raw chocolate-chip-
cookie dough. It was delicious!
We thought we'd get stomachaches,
but we were fine. I don't think there's raw eggs in there.
I've always wanted to eat a whole roll
of raw chocolate-chip-cookie dough, you know?
It was my dream come true."

All of a sudden, I see I have
Parker's full attention.
He's not staring at the ceiling anymore.
He's gazing right into my eyes
with his mouth parted.
He's breathing heavily.

"Are you okay?" I ask.

"There's a way," he says in a low voice.

"A way to what?" I ask.

The spell breaks.
Parker looks away.

"Nothing," he says
and rolls over on his side.

Parker

It takes three dozen roses to make a dent in how badly I feel about the way I treated Julianne.

"Oh, hi," she says with a frown when I show up with them on her door step.

I reach for her right hand, and she lets me have it, and I slowly kiss each finger.

"Can I drive you to school tomorrow?" I ask.

I know this is what couples are supposed to do. If a guy has a car, he's supposed to drive his girlfriend to school and back every day.

She gives me a small smile. "Okay," she says.

"I'm really sorry, Julianne," I say, extending the roses to her.

She bends over them and breathes deeply. "It's okay." She leans forward and kisses my cheek. "Want to stay for dinner?"

I stiffen immediately.

"What's the matter?"

"Nothing," I say automatically, shoving my hands into my pockets. "I, um, can't. I have youth group tonight."

"Oh," she says.

"Can I see you afterward?" I ask, even though I have homework and a test and a paper. None of it matters without Julianne.

She hesitates.

"Please," I say.

I would add, if I could say it out loud:

You're the only thing keeping me alive.

"Okay," she says.

Danielle

Parker takes us to Starbucks
after Teen Tzedakah Project
and it's great to walk in there
with him, Foxy, Amber,
and all the other cool seniors,
and have everyone notice us.

Parker asks me what I want,
and orders my vanilla latte and orange cupcake,
and waits around by the oval serving table,
where the barista yells out your order when it's ready,
and then Parker brings them right over to me.

He sits down between me and Rachel
and Rachel's face is so reddened
she looks like a cherry tomato.

She keeps touching him on the wrist.
I know she's totally freaked
by being this close to him
and I know he's being nice to her,
laughing at her jokes, answering her questions,
because she's my friend
and, at that moment, it doesn't matter
that sometimes I can't breathe
when my brother's around
because I feel smothered,
blank and faded
like an old black-and-white movie
next to a bright Technicolor one.

Sitting next to him now,
in this crowded Starbucks
with everyone looking at us
and him making sure I
have everything I need,
I feel amazing.

Today, my postcard would say:

Dear Parker,
Big brothers are nice to have.
Love,
Danielle

Parker

Myrna Katz and Associates are on the telephone when I arrive for my scheduled appointment, but Myrna motions me inside, so I take my usual seat in front of her desk.

"Tell her to join Habitat for Humanity," Myrna says into her headset. "Tell her to sign up to help Hurricane Katrina victims in Mississippi."

I stare at Myrna's "98% Track Record" sign and wonder, for the first time, about the other 2 percent. What happens to them?

"Sorry about that, Parker," Myrna says, putting down her headset. "Still haven't tried the sushi platter downstairs? Hey—have you lost weight?"

"No."

She folds her hands on the desk in front of her. "So, how we doin'?"

How we doin'? Well, Myrna, here's how we're doin'...

My calc grades are in the toilet (pun intended).

I'm in danger of losing—or may have already lost—my number-one spot to Amber Weinstein.

I missed the last few meetings of forensics, Key Club, peer leadership, and Make-A-Wish Foundation.

I'm dating a shiksa and haven't told my parents.

My father has a rare form of male breast cancer.

I like vomiting.

So how we doin'?

The truth is, my carefully constructed life—the one you so meticulously crafted for me in the last four years with a big stack of my parents' money—is falling apart.

But, instead, I smile, and I say, "Everything's fine."

Danielle

I stop Foxy in the hall
on my way to Western Civ
and tell him I want to
write poetry for *The Cellar*.

"Okay," he says.
"We meet on Tuesdays."
Then he asks, "Is Parker okay?
He's been acting kinda weird lately."

"Why is it always about Parker?"
I ask
with an edge in my voice
that I didn't mean to be there.

Foxy's eyes grow as large as UFOs.
"Um, okay, later," he says.

A part of me feels evil.
A part of me feels confused.
A part of me feels sad.
A part of me feels
tired.

Parker

The problem is that nobody pays attention.

They see what they want to see. They believe what they want to believe.

If Aaron Rosenthal let me, this is what I would write about in the new teen section of the *New Jersey Jewish Ledger*.

This is how I would start it:

Rot

By Parker Rabinowitz

In Environmental Club last year, a naturalist from the U.S. Forest Service talked to us about rot.

He said sometimes trees can look healthy on the outside, but actually be dying inside. These trees fall unexpectedly during a storm.

You see an Ivy-league-bound, athletic, straight-A future physician.

Trees aren't the only things that rot.

Danielle

I'm in my room writing a poem.
I've always wanted to write a poem.
I think this poem will be about
always being in second place.

There's a knock on my door.
"Parker?" I say in shock.

He stands there for a minute
without saying anything.
"Um," he finally says.
"I just thought ... never mind."
He walks away.

My first instinct is to jump up
and run after him
and ask, "Are you okay, Parker?

What's wrong?
What did you want to tell me?
What's the matter?
How can I help you?"

Instead, I work on my poem again
about always being in second place.

I don't want to be in pom-poms or flags,
I don't want to go to medical school,
I don't want to see a college consultant,
I don't want to be someone's little sister.

I want to be me,
not anybody else.

Dear Parker,
Big brothers may be nice to have.
But being a little sister is hard.
Love,
Danielle

Parker

Dad schedules our first-ever Family Movie Night in the home-theater room.

"We're going to watch *Exodus* together," he says.

"Why *Exodus*?" Danielle asks.

"Why not?" Dad replies. "It's got everything… action, adventure, Jewish history, romance." He nudges Danielle's elbow. She giggles.

"Does anyone want popcorn?" Mom asks. "I just made it. Peanut butter."

Everyone eagerly accepts a bowl of Mom's homemade peanut butter popcorn except me.

"You're sure, Parker?" she asks.

"He's an athlete," Dad says, popping a handful into his mouth. "He needs to make weight."

Mom nods knowingly. As if she understands.

We take our seats, Dad next to Mom, placing his arm around her. He winces as he does this. The movie rolls.

I've seen *Exodus*. Every Jewish kid in religious school has to watch it sometime. It's a good movie, but I could be studying calc, working on the new teen section of the *New Jersey Jewish Ledger*, or doing any variety of homework.

"Not too many Jews who look like that," Dad observes when Paul Newman appears on-screen.

"Parker does," Danielle says. "He looks exactly like that."

"Well, Parker's our resident Aryan," Dad says, slapping my knee. "Right, pardner? That's why we named him 'Parker.' He's special."

I say nothing, but Danielle frowns slightly in my direction.

Dad goes on, "When I was twelve, my father told me I could change my name if I wanted—shorten it, Anglicize it—but I decided to keep it. It was quite a thing, hearing 'David Rabinowitz' called at Princeton."

"So why didn't you give Parker a Jewish name?" Danielle asks.

"Because Parker's different," Dad says.

"He's not different," she says.

"We're missing the movie," I say, not because I care about the movie, but because I want them to shut up about me.

138

"Do you have a cold, Parker?" Mom asks. "Your voice is really hoarse."

I cough. "Yeah, I do."

We don't speak for the rest of the movie. By the middle of it, Dad's fast asleep, snoring by my head.

Danielle

"Do you think Mom and Dad
would let me go out with a non-Jewish boyfriend?"

"I don't know," Parker answers.

"When are you going to tell them
about Julianne?"

"I don't know."

"Do you think you're special?"

"No."

"Do you think you're different?"

"No."

"Nobody pays attention to me.
They only pay attention to you."

I'm being mean to Parker again,
but I shouldn't be
because it's not his fault
that he's so beautiful and smart
and special and different
and gifted and talented.

"Sometimes," he says,
"it's better not to have attention."

"Are you okay, Parker?" I ask.
"You seem really tired.
You can talk to me, you know.
You can talk to me anytime."

I want to help Parker.
I really do.
I want to be a good sister.
Not a mean one.

He stares at me for so long
that I feel hypnotized.
It's not till he releases me
that I dare blink.

"It's nothing," he says.

Parker

I binge and purge every day now.

It seems like just the other day I was doing it only a few times a week and now I can't miss a single day.

I can't stop.

Danielle

Dad has a mastectomy.
Why? Why my dad?

How is it possible for a man to have breast cancer?
And why is it my dad who does?
Why him
of all the dads in the world?

Nobody talks about it. Ever.
The only thing that even reminds me
that Dad has breast cancer
are Mom's trips with him to the cancer center.

I feel horrible to admit this
but sometimes I even forget about it.

And sometimes
I wish I could forget about it.

Parker

Why do I not care as much as I should about Dad's breast cancer?

Why?

Because it's strange?

Because I have my own problems?

Because ... he might die?

Even though no one talks about it, information is not in short supply. There are brochures all around the house, as if to prevent any awkward questions. In 2007, 2,030 new cases of invasive breast cancer were diagnosed among men in the United States. Breast cancer accounts for 0.22 percent (two tenths of a percent) of cancer deaths among men.

I thought I wanted to be a doctor.

Why am I not more interested in Dad's treatments,

talking to his doctors, reading about his cancer, learning more, knowing more?

Why is it that I've never gone to the cancer center with him and Mom?

For the first time, I think back to the warning Myrna Katz and Associates gave me on my first day in her office, about whose goals I was satisfying by wanting to go to med school.

Danielle

Somebody pukes in the cafeteria today.

I can't blame them.
They did serve Sloppy Joes in the cafeteria today.

I watch the janitor clean up the puke.
First, he swabs it away with paper towels.
Then he squirts the floor with a detergent
that smells like lemons.
Then he wipes the floor with more paper towels.
Then he squirts the floor with ammonia
and washes the area with his trusty mop.

He whistles throughout
the washing and wiping and squirting and mopping.

He's having fun.
He's having fun cleaning up puke.

He's happy
because he accomplished something
important today.

That makes me smile.

Parker

Mom is the chairperson of the New Jersey Jewish Music Festival. Their opening event is a recreated 1930s radio program, *It Don't Mean a Thing If It Ain't Yiddish Swing*, at the Bickford Theater in the Morris Museum. She's been planning it for two years.

A hundred people mill around the museum lobby holding champagne flutes, while waiters walk around offering trays of finger food. Some of the women are in gowns and some of the men are in tuxedos. Everyone's talking and laughing and eating and drinking.

All of us are there except Dad. He's still in the hospital.

Mom was there for his surgery, and we're going there tomorrow, but it feels wrong for us to be partying it up here while he's there.

I wonder if, in the 1930s, people's priorities were this screwed up.

"How does it look up there?" Mom asks me, nodding at the stage and wringing her hands. She spent months working on the stage design. She spent even more time working on her outfit.

"It's nice," I say distractedly. "Shouldn't we be at the hospital?"

Mom stiffens. "Like I said, we'll go tomorrow." She looks down at her fancy shoes. "Your dad wanted us to be here."

"Why?" Danielle asks with her mouth furrowed into a deep scowl.

Mom blinks furiously. "To keep up appearances," she whispers. She looks away. "Excuse me for a minute."

She flees into the ladies' room. Danielle runs after her.

I end up watching the show by myself.

Danielle

I hate hospitals.

I hate the smell
I hate the people.

I know they try to make it friendly-like
with the nurses wearing green-and-purple paisley
and the plush sea-foam carpeting
and the paintings of grapes on the walls
and the shiny glass sculptures in the waiting room
and the fountains in the lobby.

But it's not friendly.

Dad's doing well.
That's what his doctors say.
He doesn't look well to me.
He looks pale and skinny.

He looks like
I could knock him over
just by blowing on him.

His eyes are closed.
He doesn't talk.
I don't even think he knows we're here.

Mom's in a chair by Dad's bed
in an ugly sweat suit,
not her sparkly periwinkle suit
with matching freshwater pearls
that she wore to the Yiddish show
even though she spent the whole three hours
in the handicapped stall
crying
while I sat on the cold floor
next to her.

She looked nice then
even though she was sad.
Now she looks ugly and sad.

Parker's sitting in a chair in the corner
staring at his sneakers
so intently
it's as if the secrets of the universe
are imprinted on them.

He's as pale and skinny
as Dad.
I could knock him over too
just by blowing on him.

I look past Dad
out the window
at a gray sky,
a black-tar roof,
and an ugly parking lot.

I wanted to come.
Now I wish I could leave.

Everything is
sick,
sad,
and
ugly.

Parker

My alarm rings at 5:00 a.m., but I don't get up till 7:00 a.m. It's the first time I can remember not beating my alarm.

Dad asked me at the hospital yesterday to keep going to minyan without him, but I've missed it by oversleeping.

I pick up Julianne at her house. She slides into my car and instead of giving me a huge kiss like she usually does, she says, "Oh, Parker, you don't look so good. Your face is almost … yellow. Are you okay?"

"It's nothing!" I snap. "I'm fine, okay?"

I'm instantly sorry, when all she did was ask me if I was okay, but I don't apologize.

We drive to school in silence. Before it was renovated in 1999, Livingstone High School was nothing special, but today it has a green-trimmed brick façade and glass atrium like the Short Hills Mall does. The digital sign out front brags about it being named one of the best schools in the United States by *Newsweek* magazine.

I want to run away from this place. Right now, as far as I can get, with Julianne, and never come back. But instead, like a pre-programmed good-kid robot, I pull into the parking lot. When I finally turn to look at Julianne, I see she's crying quietly.

She opens her door and races away. I chase her and shout, even though it rips my throat apart, "Julianne! Julianne! I'm sorry! I'm sorry!"

She stops. She looks up at me, crying, and says, "You're so moody all the time, Parker, and you never tell me anything. I ... I don't think you really like me."

"No. No," I say. "I love you. I need you."

She sniffles loudly. "I love you too, Parker, but ... you're so hard to get along with." She gives me a pleading look. "Please tell me what's wrong."

I think about it. I think about telling her everything.

I reply, "Nothing's wrong. Why does everyone keep asking me that?"

Danielle

Any news involving McDreamy
always travels fast at Livingstone.
Rachel, for one, seems delirious with joy
about my brother and Julianne breaking up.

"I'll bake him mint brownies," she says to me.
"I'll bring them over tonight.
They're my specialty."

How totally dumb.
Mint brownies aren't going to help anything
no matter whose specialty they are.

My first thought
is the same one I always have.
Is Rachel my friend because of Parker?

My second thought is that

I'm ashamed by my first thought.
I wish I could pretend I never had it.
But it rips up my insides.

Parker

I go to her locker at the end of the day. She looks up at me with pink-rimmed eyes.

"I wish it had worked out," she whispers. "Really."

"Please, Julianne," I beg, my voice cracking. "Give me another chance."

Would it help if I got down on my knees? Because I'd do it in a minute.

"I gave you so many chances," she says, sniffling. "I think ... deep inside ... you just don't want me."

"No. No," I say fiercely, taking her hands. "That isn't true. It's ... It's ..."

She takes a step toward me. "It's what, Parker? Why can't you tell me?"

I lower my eyes. Neither of us moves. Then she pulls her hands out of mine and walks away.

Danielle

Even though it's not my place,
I tell Mom about Parker.

"His girlfriend, Julianne," I say.
"I think she dumped him.
I think he's really upset about it."

"I'm sorry, sweetie," Mom says,
rushing from one end of the bedroom
to the other, looking for her sensible brown shoes.
"I can't talk right now. I have to pick
up your father at the cancer center.
I'm late."

Mom's distracted.
Everyone's distracted.
Everyone's always distracted.

Dear Parker,
I'm starting to understand
a little.
How does a person get attention?
By doing something big
dramatic
show-stopping.
Sometimes
it's the only way
to count.

At least
above
nothing.

Love,
Danielle

Parker

I go to her house after school.

"Please," I say, putting my hand on her waist. "If you just knew..."

"If I just knew what?" she says. "What is it?"

I take a step closer. "I love you, Julianne."

"I don't think you really do," she says. "I don't think you ever did."

She closes the door in my face.

Danielle

Mom and Dad are getting ready to go
to the Denim and Diamonds Gala
for Pony Power Therapies
even though Dad's lying in bed
in his black tuxedo and black cowboy boots
with his eyes closed
while Mom fixes her hair
under her tan-and-teal cowboy hat.

"Why don't you just stay home?" I ask them.

"We go every year," Dad answers faintly.
"People will wonder."

"So what?" I ask, my voice sounding impatient.
Dad doesn't answer.
Mom doesn't answer.

I gaze at Dad's hand
resting along the brim of his cowboy hat
next to him on the bed.
It's looks like an old man's hand.
Pale and blue-veined.

I get up and go to Parker's room.
"This family needs help," I say,
but stop myself abruptly in his doorway,
because Parker's lying on his bed
exactly like Dad
with his eyes closed, too.

"Why am I the only person around here
who thinks anything's wrong?" I ask,
plopping down next to him on the bed.

Parker opens one eye.
"Because you're smart, Danielle," he says.
"You see what other people don't see."

"Your teeth, Parker," I whisper.
"They're so gray."

Parker shuts his mouth
and his eyes
and himself.

Parker

I do something I've never done before.

I vomit in the school bathroom after Key Club and before National Honor Society.

And I know, from now on, it's going to be twice a day.

Danielle

What am I supposed to do?
Who am I supposed to talk to?
What am I supposed to say?

You can call 911 when you hurt yourself.
But who do you call
when your family's hurting itself?

Is there an ambulance?
An emergency room?
A pill to pop?

I'm confused.
And scared.

If someone would just tell me
what to do
I would do it.

I want to help.
I just don't know how.

Dear Parker,
You're so smart.
Please tell me what I should do.
Love,
Danielle

Parker

After our laps today, Coach lines us up like soldiers and walks up and down the line yelling at us.

"Lay off the Krispy Kremes, Grossman."

"Yessir."

"Getting paunchy around the middle."

"Yessir."

"How do you expect to win carrying that tire around?"

"Yessir."

"Stay away from fryers."

"Yessir."

"I want you to do extra laps for me."

"Yessir."

My hands start to sweat.

Am I going to be next? Is Coach going to ream me out for being fat?

Coach stops right in front of me. He looks me up and down, then frowns.

Why can't I lose weight?

When will I stop being a failure?

That's it. I need to stop screwing around.

When I get home, I run around our block again and again, over and over, one lap after another, until I'm panting, until I can hardly breathe, until I feel dizzy.

I limp home, I barely make it up the stairs, and I collapse into bed.

The room is spinning wildly.

I wish it would stop.

I want to cry, because I feel so bad.

Danielle

I try to talk to Rachel about things
one afternoon
when we're working
on our poems for *The Cellar*.

"Has your brother lost weight?"
she asks.
"He looks skinny."

"I don't know," I say.
I close my mouth,
then open it,
then close and open it again.

I ask, "Do you ever wonder
what people are hiding?"

"What are you talking about?"

she snaps.

"Nothing," I say.

"We have to work on our poems," she says.

So we do.
Here's mine:

Secrets
Some secrets are good.
Some are bad.
They aren't easy to keep
but they're even harder
to tell.

Parker

I heard Dad vomiting in the bathroom today. It must be his treatments.

I peeked inside and saw Mom standing behind him, telling him it would be okay, stroking his hair.

Like me.

And not like me.

Danielle

Parker and I are on our own for dinner.
We order an extra-large pizza called
"Everything But the Kitchen Sink"
from The Tomato Pie Factory.

It has cheese, olives, sausage, peppers, onions,
mushrooms, eggplant, chicken, pepperoni,
pineapple, and maraschino cherries.
Parker has five slices.

"Wish I could eat that much," I say.

"I need to lose a few pounds," he says.

"Get real," I say.

"I'm fat," he says.

Something hot and cold—both at the same time—smack
    me in the forehead
like a burning-icy-headache.

Parker gets up.
"Parker?" I call.

He doesn't answer.
He goes to the bathroom.
He closes the door and locks it.

I hear water
running fiercely in the sink,
and
gagging.
It can't be.
Is that . . .
Is he . . .

"Parker!"
I bang on the door.
"Parker!"

After what seems like an eternity,
Parker opens the door.

"What are you doing?" I ask.
"I'm not *doing* anything," he says, walking away from me.

I grab the back of his shirt. "But why are you doing that?"
He peels my hand off. "Don't worry about me, Danielle. It's nothing."

Parker

I go to a party tonight with Foxy and Spaz, even though I want to stay home. I feel so tired.

It's while we're driving over that I start feeling like I want to tell them. I've never wanted anything so much in my life.

"Do you guys ever do … anything … when you're up-set … about something?"

I'm not sure this is the right way to begin, but I can't think of any other way.

"I eat chocolate," Spaz says.

"I eat babes," Foxy says.

"Chocolate?"

"Yeah, I'm just like a girl," Spaz says. "Food is my com-fort, dude."

I'm sorry I brought it up. But I force myself to go on.

"Do you ever eat … a lot? Like … a whole lot?"

174

Spaz lets out a laugh. "Are you kidding? You're looking at Porky Pig over here. I'm no slacker when it comes to binging."

Binging?

I don't know how to respond. I'm not even sure I should respond. But, before I can make up my mind what to say, we arrive at the party. Well, it was a dumb idea, anyway.

All the popular kids from my school, and some really hot girls from Schechter, are lounging around the living room listening to music. I sit down in a corner by myself. Spaz sits across from me, next to Amber, and they start kissing, and it makes me think of Julianne and how much I miss her, and I stare at them fiercely, but they're so wrapped up in their kiss they don't even notice.

I'm invisible.

The conversation turns to "last meals."

"My last meal would be a soft, warm, chocolate-chip cookie with a cold glass of milk," says Amber.

"Mine would be steak," says Foxy.

"Pizza," says Tina.

"How about you, Parker?" Spaz asks.

I feel like every meal is my last. Before I can come up with an answer, someone says, "Parker's last meal would be a crumb."

"Well," one of the hot girls puts in, and I realize it's the same girl from the Teen Tzedakah Project. "Maybe that's why he's got a great body." She looks right at me. I look back at her, then away.

"Leave the guy alone," Foxy snaps.

I wish I could tell him. Or even Spaz. Why can't I? Why can't I ask for help?

The conversation shifts again, and I stare at Spaz and Amber again, only this time he catches me looking at him.

"Are you okay?" he asks.

Do I have a sign around my neck that says

This Loser Needs Your Immediate Attention!

"Why are you looking at me like that?"

Spaz averts his eyes. "It's just … Have you lost weight? You look skinny."

"No."

By the end of the night, the hot girl who said I had a great body winds up in my lap. Turns out her name is Chelsea Levine. We've been making out pretty vigorously for the past fifteen minutes, but it isn't me she's making out with, because I'm not really here.

Danielle

I don't know what to do about Parker.
What's happening to him?

I make a list of all the people I could ask for help:
1. Rabbi Goldwasser (but I haven't talked to him since my bat mitzvah)
2. Aaron Rosenthal (but he gives me the creeps)
3. My homeroom teacher (but I don't think that's gonna work)
4. The school principal (but I've never even seen her)
5. The school nurse (but I don't even know where her office is)
6. Parker's track coach (but he gives me the creeps even more than Aaron Rosenthal)
7. Rachel's mom (but she's just like Rachel, only worse)

I study my list for a long time

and then I add:
8. Mom
9. Dad

Then I tear it into small pieces
and throw it in the garbage.

Parker

"Parker?"

It's Danielle standing in my doorway. I tell her to come in. She sits down on the bed next to me and stares at my face. I look away quickly.

"Your eyes," she murmurs. "They're so ... sunken." She touches my cheek. "And your face is so thin." Her eyes fill with tears. "What are you doing to yourself? Whatever it is, Parker, please stop it."

"I'm not doing anything," I say, and it comes out so hoarse I sound like the Godfather.

Danielle gets a desperate look in her eyes. "I'll tell them," she whispers.

I barely have the energy to keep my eyes open, but I sit up and seize her arm. Hard. My fingers leave a red mark on her skin.

"Don't you dare, Danielle, don't you dare tell anyone."

"You know I'll never tell," she sobs. "But please stop it, Parker, just stop it."

I can't.

Danielle

Rachel wants to watch a movie after school
in our home-theater room.
I give her the list Mom made
of all the movies we own.

"Is *Singin' in the Rain* any good?"
she asks.

"Yeah, it's good," I say.
"It's happy and there's a lot of dancing."

"How about *The Band Wagon*?"
"Same."
"*Seven Brides for Seven Brothers*?"
"Same."
"*The Music Man*?"
"They're all the same!

They're all happy and
… unrealistic!"

Rachel rolls her eyes. "What's your problem?"

I look away. "Just pick the stupid movie.
It doesn't matter.
It totally doesn't matter."

Dear Parker,
Remember when we watched *The Music Man* together?
Are we going to do that again?
You were still with Julianne.
Dad was still okay.
My biggest problem was
not playing paintball.
Are
you
ever
coming
back?
Love,
Danielle

Parker

I have to lose weight. That will bring Julianne back to me.

I get up in the middle of the night and drive to a twenty-four-hour Wal-Mart in the next county.

It's close to three o'clock in the morning and the aisles are empty. I walk up and down the pharmacy section, then stop in front of the laxatives display.

But I have no money. I spent everything on my food last week.

I grab a few boxes off the shelf, stuff them into my jacket, and quickly walk out of the store.

Danielle

I see Julianne in the hall
right before lunch
and I almost want to run up to her
and tell her
but where would I start?

Beginning 1
You broke Parker's heart. He loved you. You're the only girl
  he ever crushed, and now look what you've done.

Beginning 2
Parker has a problem. Can you help him? He loves you.

Beginning 3
Will you please get back together with my brother? I
  don't know if that will solve his problem, but I know
  it will help.

Beginning 4

What's your family like? Are your parents around or are they at this gala and that exhibit and this reception and that fundraiser?

Beginning 5

I'm afraid for my brother. Really, really afraid.

Parker

Dad remembers to pay me this week, so I go to the supermarket and buy more food to hide in my closet. I spend it all, $350, loading two shopping carts.

"Hey, you're here a lot," the cashier says. "Buying for the U.S. Army or something?"

I shrug in response, but her comments freak me out totally.

When I get home, I vomit for the third time that day.

Danielle

I can't take it.
I have to say it out loud.

"Something's wrong."

Mom and Dad look up at me,
with their forks frozen in midair.
It's the first time all of us
have had dinner together as a family
in two and a half weeks.

"What's wrong?" Mom asks.

"Everything," I say. "Dad's sick
but everyone's pretending he's not."

Something in Dad's eyes tells me
I've crossed a line,
but almost half a second later,

so quickly I think maybe I imagined it,
he answers in a silky-smooth tone,
the kind his secretary calls his honey voice,
"Nobody's pretending anything, sweetheart."
"There's something else," I say.

Parker smashes my foot under the table.
I let out a yelp.

"What?" Mom asks.

"Nothing," I mumble.

We go back to eating
as if
I never said anything at all.

The walls of our dining room
are covered with grotesque African masks
that we picked up on safari in Kenya two years ago.
That's how I feel,
like I'm wearing a mask,
a mask that hides all this secret ugliness,
turning it inside,
forcing me to swallow it instead.

Parker

"Dude! We're going bowling!"

The mere thought of picking up a bowling ball makes me want to lie down.

"I'm kind of tired tonight," I say.

I can hear Foxy's impatience on the other end of the line. "Come on, Parker, you need to get out."

"I'm just too tired," I say. I barely have the energy to get up in the mornings.

He gives up. "Okay. But you don't know what you're missing."

My life's falling apart.

But, as long as I can do that thing three times a day, it's okay.

Danielle

I want things to be the way they used to be.
When did they get like this?
Were they always like this?

I know it has something to do with Dad's cancer
and Parker's problem.

But I have a feeling
things started way before that.

Like maybe when we had this
huge house built or
when Mom quit her job at Goldman Sachs,
so she could be chairperson
of this committee and that council.

Or maybe it started much earlier than that.

Maybe it started when Dad

went to Princeton
and decided Parker
should go there too.

Parker

I manage to go all day without eating a single thing, but I'm starving by the time I get home.

When I look in my closet, I see I've run out of food.

I have no money.

I jump in my car, drive to the huge Wawa off the interstate that's always crowded with truckers, and while the cashiers are busy ringing up lottery tickets and cigarettes, I stuff seven candy bars into my jacket. I notice there's a lot more space in my jacket than I thought, so I stuff three more in it, and walk out.

Add "thief" to the list of things I don't look like. I get away with it again.

Danielle

"Mom, I have to talk to you."

"Oh, sweetie, I'm really late for your dad's appointment."

"You're so busy!
You don't pay attention!"

"What's this about, Danielle?
Is it about your dad?"

"It's ... It's ... "

"I don't have a lot of time, sweetie."

"Fine! Go!"

I run up the stairs, slam my door,
and hope Mom will follow me there.

But she doesn't.

Parker

I get dizzy all the time now.

My stomach's been hurting.

My throat feels raw.

The other day, I think I saw blood in my vomit.

I'm running and fasting and using laxatives and vomiting four times a day.

But I'm still not getting skinnier.

I have to vary where I shop for food. The cashiers recognize me, and they make comments about how much I buy.

I drove almost two hours out of my way last night so I could shop at a different supermarket.

Danielle

"Danielle?"
"Yes."
"Myrna Katz. How are you?"
"Fine."
"Is Parker home?"
"Um, no. Can I take a message for him?"
"He missed his last appointment
and he hasn't been returning calls to his cell."

Pause.
"Danielle?"
"Yeah?"
"Is your mom or dad home?"
"No."

Pause.
"Can you ask them to call me?"

Parker

I'm walking to AP Physics with Amber when an overwhelming sensation of dizziness makes me trip over my feet.

"Parker?"

I realize I've crumpled against Amber, and she's struggling to hold up my weight. I force myself to stand, clawing at the water fountain to steady myself.

"What happened?" she whispers. "Are you okay? I'll take you to the school nurse."

"No," I say hoarsely. "I'm okay now."

She fastens me with frantic eyes. "What's happening to you, Parker?"

I swallow hard, feeling a cold sweat come over me. "Nothing. I just need...a minute."

Amber holds me tighter. "Parker, you've lost weight."

"No," I say, my voice gaining in strength. I straighten up and shrug her off. "No, I haven't."

Danielle

"You have bulimia."
"What?" Parker asks.

"It's an eating disorder.
Mostly girls have it.
You're sick, Parker."

"No, I'm not."

"Yes, you are!
You need help.
Look at you!
You can't even stand up!"

He puts his hands over his ears.
"Shut up," he says.

I start to cry.
"But I want to help you. You need help."

He grabs my shoulders
and shakes me hard.
"Don't you dare tell anyone!
Don't—tell—anyone!"

He won't stop shaking me
until I finally whimper,
"Okay, Parker, okay."

Parker

Track meet.
>   Hungry.
>   Tired.
>   Can't think.
>   Dad here?
>   "Have fun."
>   What?
>   Jerk with starter's gun.
>   Drives blue Ford Bronco.
>   Hate blue Ford Broncos.
>   Gets out, looks at watch, pulls out gun, fires, back in car, leaves.
>   Stomach cramps.
>   Dad hugs me.

Danielle

I pick up the phone
three times
and hang up
three times.

On my fourth try
I stay on.
But her cell must be turned off.

"Hi, um, Myrna," I say.
"It's Danielle.
Danielle Rabinowitz.
Parker's sister?
Um, I need to tell you something.
It's really important.
Can you call me?"

Parker

I stay after school and run around the track for so long I almost pass out twice.

All I want to do is crawl into bed. I drive home, get out of the car, and limp into the house, but I don't know if I'll make it up the stairs. Before I can get to my room, though, I hear loud voices, and Mom and Dad suddenly appear on the landing in front of me.

Dad's waving a piece of paper around. "You didn't get in!" he screams. "You didn't get into Princeton!"

"For goodness sake, David!" Mom shouts back. "Nothing he does is ever good enough for you!"

Track, forensics, youth group, peer leadership, Make-A-Wish Foundation, Student Council, SAT prep classes, AP classes... All my efforts of the last four years to get into the college of Dad's choice whirl around me like the remnants of a last meal being flushed down a dark drain.

I go into my room because I have to lie down, I have to, but Dad follows me, so I leave and go into the bathroom, my sanctuary, but Dad follows me in there too, and he's still screaming, and mom's still screaming.

Knees buckle.

Smack.

Convulsing.

Dad kneels.

"Call an ambulance!

Oh, Parker, no."

Black.

Danielle

Do you know how many chances I had?

I will never forgive myself.

Or Mom.
Or Dad.

Or Parker.

Parker

I wake up in the hospital.

At first I'm surprised.

Then I'm relieved.

I have all kinds of tubes in me—food tubes, breathing tubes—I think I even have a tube for going to the bathroom.

I had a seizure. I almost died.

They won't let me vomit here. And they force me to eat.

I think I've gained weight.

Danielle

In the doctor's dimly lit office in the hospital,
the doctor says,
"Your son is bulimic."

Dad: "What?"
Mom: (cries quietly into a tissue).
Dad: "But isn't that ... "
Mom: (cries quietly into a tissue).
Dad: "But he's a boy ... "
Mom: (cries quietly into a tissue).

I don't say, "I told you so."
I don't say anything.

Mom turns to Dad
and sobs, "It's just like ... your cancer."

"Except that Dad got help," I say.

205

"And Parker didn't."

They both stare at me.

Then Dad cries.

Parker

Foxy and Spaz pull up chairs and sit close. Amber holds my hand.

"I should've known," she says, her voice cracking. "I should've helped."

"We all should've helped," Spaz says.

"We all should've known," Foxy says.

How could they have known?

I didn't even know.

"Parker," Spaz says, looking down at the floor. "I … I … "

We all wait for him to finish.

"I'm sorry," he finally says, looking at me.

I finally know what I was chosen for.

Danielle

"Why didn't you tell me?"
Rachel asks.
"My cousin had bulimia.
We could've talked."
She hugs me close.
"I care," she says.

I think of that list I made
of all the people I could've asked for help.
Rachel's mom was on it,
but Rachel wasn't.

Sometimes things are so obvious
they stare you right in the face
and you still can't see them.

Not listening.

Not seeing.
Not paying attention.

I did it too.

Parker

Julianne cries, and says over and over, "I didn't know, I didn't know, I didn't know."

Before she leaves, she kisses me and says, "I love you so much, Parker, and when you forgive me—if you forgive me—I'll be waiting for you."

Danielle

In Parker's hospital room
there's always a lot of crying,
a lot of apologizing,
even some joking,
and, finally, some talking.

Mom says things like,
"I should've noticed.
I can't believe I didn't.
Or maybe I did.
But I didn't see."

Dad says things like,
"First male breast cancer.
Now male bulimia.
We're two very special guys, pardner."
Nobody laughs.

But we know it's just Dad's way.
At least he's trying.

It isn't always easy
to hear these things
or say them
but it's better than
that horrible silence.
That was like a heavy blanket,
dark and choking,
covering everything up.

This is like a blanket unfurled.
Kicking up dust,
making you gag and cough,
but at least it lets in light.

Parker doesn't talk much.
Neither do I.
I write him another postcard.

Dear Parker,
No matter how ugly something is,
it's better to see it than not see it.
Besides, beauty can be deceiving.
Love,
Danielle
P.S. I was wrong. You're not worse than a girl.

Parker

They're letting me go home tomorrow.

I know things will be different.

A part of me feels good about that. Another part of me doesn't.

I know I can't have my old life back.

I also know I can do better.

And I don't mean by being perfect.

Danielle

Parker's coming home.
I wrote a poem for him:

Who Are You?
Just because you break hearts
  doesn't make you a heartbreaker.
Just because you get straight As
  doesn't make you a success.
Just because you have a college consultant
  doesn't make you college-bound.
Just because you fail to act
  doesn't make you cowardly.
Just because you need help
  doesn't make you weak.
Just because the world sees you as something
  or as nothing

doesn't mean anything
at all.

Parker folds it carefully into his pocket.
"I'll always keep it with my breath mints,"
he says. He winks at me.
"And I'll publish it in the *New Jersey Jewish Ledger.*"

Parker

I have a shrink. His name is Dr. Morrow. He tells me I have abnormally low self-esteem.

"That means you don't think very highly of yourself," he says.

He must think I can't understand this, because he tries to bring it down to my level.

"You think you're a loser. When you're actually quite the opposite."

He continues. "You have a distorted body image, Parker. Your self-esteem is all wrapped up in your weight and appearance and body image. When you look in the mirror, it's like you're in a funhouse. You see someone fat, and no matter how much weight you lose, no matter how skinny you get, you'll always see someone fat, until … there's nothing left of you. Until … you're … gone."

This gets my attention.

"We have a lot of work to do, Parker. We're going to change this distorted body image. We're going to rebuild your self-esteem. We're going to teach you about nutrition, healthy eating, forming a better relationship with food. We're going to show you how to express your feelings. We're going to teach you better ways to cope with stress than by binging and purging. Are you ready to work on all these things, Parker?"

"Yes," I say.

I mean it.

Danielle

My poem wins the Ida and Max Cohen Award
for New Voices in Literature by Jewish Teens.

Mom and Dad make a big deal out of it.
Dad hangs my plaque in the living room.
Mom frames my poem next to it.
It's the first time I've ever won anything.

The first time I've earned first place.

Parker takes me out to dinner.
To the Japanese restaurant
under Myrna Katz and Associates.

"I hear the spicy salmon rolls
are to die for," he says with a wink.

Parker

I still binge sometimes. Dr. Morrow calls them relapses. He says they're okay. He says I shouldn't beat myself up over them.

But, even though I binge, I don't purge anymore.

Purging hurt me. The acid from my stomach wore out the enamel on my teeth, tore up my esophagus, and nearly gave me an ulcer. It messed up the electrolyte balance in my body, because every time I threw up, I got rid of important stuff my body needed, like potassium, chloride, and sodium. It screwed up my blood sugar and my metabolism.

I failed AP Calculus.

I didn't get into HYP.

In a few weeks, everyone will go off to college, except me. I'm taking time off.

We're all taking time off.

Dad's okay. He's in remission. He makes a point of talking to me every day.

It's not always significant. Sometimes it's just about the weather.

Today, though, he says, "We're in a class all by ourselves, Parker, you and me. We're medical miracles, statistical sensations, disease deviants."

I'm used to Dad's jokes about our cancer and bulimia being "girl things." Mom says making fun of them is his way of accepting them.

Dad's expression gets serious. "It's not true," he says softly. "What I told you about success and failure."

"I know," I say.

He hugs me close. I hug him back.

Like Dad, I'll never be totally cured.

I'll always have issues with food.

Every day, I ignore the voice inside me that tells me I'm fat, I'm a failure, I'm worthless.

I'll have to live with this for the rest of my life.

But I'm in a better place now.

I just need to do one more thing.

———

I ring her doorbell. She comes to the door. I ask, "Julianne, will you go out with me?"

Author's Note

Although an estimated ten million girls and women in the United States suffer from eating disorders, an estimated one million boys and men do, too. And the number of male sufferers rises every year.

One out of every four people suffering from anorexia is a male; one out of every eight people suffering from bulimia is a male. Boys and men are less likely to seek treatment because they're often too embarrassed to ask for help. Athletes—runners, swimmers, dancers, rowers, gymnasts, and wrestlers—are particularly susceptible to bulimia. Because eating disorders are so associated with females, males may tend to be overlooked when they show symptoms of them.

Bulimia is a mental disorder. Bulimics binge and purge large quantities of food, often experiencing a worsening progression of obsessive-compulsive behaviors that may include hoarding, lying, and stealing. They may also abuse laxatives and diet pills, fast, and exercise excessively.

Although the first incident of binging and purging may happen by accident, the binge-purge cycle becomes a way for bulimics to avoid feelings of anxiety, stress, depression, rejection, or intimacy. They turn to food for comfort, like many people do, but when a bulimic binges, this comfort is only temporary. Bulimics must purge to relieve themselves of the guilt of their binge. Their failure to control their binge undermines their self-esteem, and because their self-esteem is defined by their weight and appearance, a binge is the worst thing they can do to themselves. Bulimics become trapped in an endless, addictive cycle of binging and purging.

Many bulimics find the act of purging more soothing than binging, and will often binge just to purge. Why do they find purging so soothing? Several reasons: (1) it acts as a release, especially of anger; (2) it returns them to control after losing control during a binge; (3) it can be a form of self-punishment; (4) it protects them from dreaded weight gain; and (5) it frees them from dieting.

Bulimics know their behaviors are abnormal, but they don't know how to stop them. Because of this awareness, they often feel depressed, ashamed, lonely, isolated, helpless, and guilty. They avoid close relationships. Bulimia can destroy their social interactions. They suffer in secret. Like alcoholics, they usually deny it to themselves and others. Their lives often feel out of control. They try to regain control by controlling their bodies.

Bulimics usually have low self-esteem and an exaggerated need to obtain approval from others. They have distorted body images. Though bulimia affects men and women of all races and classes, bulimics tend to be high achievers and perfectionists. Their families may put pressure on them to succeed.

While anorexics—people who starve themselves—are visibly thin, bulimics may not necessarily be skinny. They can lose weight, gain weight, or fluctuate. This makes it even harder to help them.

If not stopped, bulimia can cause life-threatening conditions such as kidney damage, stomach rupture, seizures, and heart failure. Treatment for bulimia consists of behavior therapy and sometimes medication, too.

Many bulimics struggle for years or a lifetime with their disease. I compressed Parker's battle into a few months for the sake of my story.

For more information about eating disorders, please contact:

National Eating Disorders Association
www.nationaleatingdisorders.org

Academy for Eating Disorders
www.aedweb.org

Anorexia Nervosa and Related Eating Disorders, Inc.
www.anred.com

Eating Disorders Anonymous
www.eatingdisordersanonymous.org

Overeaters Anonymous
www.oa.org

© Joel L. Friedman

About the Author

Robin Friedman has worked as a children's book editor, a newspaper reporter, and an advertising copywriter. She is currently the special projects editor at the *New Jersey Jewish News*, and lives in New Jersey with her husband, Joel, and their cats, Peppercorn and Peaches. Robin has written over a hundred articles on topics such as road rage, flirting, being nice, and the prom. She is the author of *The Girlfriend Project, The Silent Witness: A True Story of the Civil War*, and *How I Survived My Summer Vacation: And Lived to Write the Story*. Visit her at robinfriedman.com.

Robin Friedman met Tom Davis at *The Daily Targum*, a college newspaper, when both were journalism students at Rutgers University. He is the real-life inspiration behind Parker Rabinowitz.

Tom is an award-winning journalist with *The Record*, a daily newspaper in New Jersey, where he wrote *Coping*, one of the nation's only columns on mental health, for five years. In 2004, he received a Rosalynn Carter Mental Health Journalism Fellowship, and in 2007, he was named Citizen of the Year by the American Psychiatric Association's New Jersey Chapter. Tom blogs about mental health issues at coping-with-life.com.

—————

RF: Why do you think eating disorders are on the rise among males?

TD: There may be a rise in cases, but it's more like a rise in reported cases.

There's always been something very shameful to men about eating disorders. It's a threat to their masculinity—a woman's disease. But mental health professionals say their eating disorder caseload is expanding largely because it's becoming more acceptable for men to come forward and admit it.

There's also a lot of ignorance. Many men still don't associate their gender with the illness. When it first happened to me, I didn't even think of eating disorders. I figured that I just had a stomach problem. All my stress goes to my stomach—I just figured that I was following my previous course of dealing with stress.

What was your perception of eating disorders prior to writing about them?

RF: I confess that I didn't know how anorexia and bulimia differed from each other. And I had no idea males suffered from either of them.

How did *Nothing* capture your experience?

TD: The loneliness. That empty feeling of losing control. That feeling of being blocked by some imaginary wall that prevents you from coming forward and sharing your problems with the world.

It's interesting how sports and running intersect with the narrative. At my lowest point, I was getting myself sick, not eating, and running five miles a day. Talk about a diet plan.

What did you feel when you first heard I had an eating disorder?

RF: Disbelief, shock, confusion. Shame and guilt, too. I tried to capture each of these emotions in *Nothing*, in the way the people in Parker's life react to his illness.

Why do so many bulimics suffer in secret?

TD: Shame. Once you start with bulimia, you get addicted to the feeling of losing it. Once you do it a few times, you feel like you can't stop. It's like being a drug addict without having to spend the money.

How did writing *Nothing* change your perception of eating disorders?

RF: I didn't realize eating disorders were less about food, more about control. I didn't know they were lifelong struggles. The most heartbreaking perception was learning that people suffer in total secrecy.

What do you think is the most misunderstood part of having bulimia?

TD: That you can't just "snap out of it." That's my least favorite phrase or idiom in the English language. I never use it with my own kids, for that reason.

People don't realize that there's no simple cure for mental illness—much like there is no simple cure for any disease that can't be eliminated with an antibiotic or vaccination.

How do you believe teens will perceive your characters? Do you think they'll be sympathetic or understanding?

RF: I hope they're sympathetic and understanding of both Parker and Danielle. I hope they're even sympathetic and understanding of Parker and Danielle's parents. Most of all, I hope *Nothing* captures that tragic loneliness that accompanies mental illness.

What do you hope teens will gain from reading *Nothing*?

TD: Understanding. I want that fifteen-year-old who's sitting in his room, wondering why his stomach is doing jumping jacks, to know: There's hope.